LOVING
ZELDA

(A STORY OF CHANGE RELUCTANTLY TOLD)

WES DEMOTT

Wes DeMott
Admiral House Publishing

For permission or further information email the publisher at:
RightsandPermissions@ AdmiralHousePublishing.com

ISBN 978-9851741-2-5
More information about the author at
http://wesdemott.com

CHAPTER 1 - The Delivery

I feel no choice but to start with an apology or, at the minimum, point out that I never intended to reveal myself so completely slit open by events beginning on February 27th, 1995. So to be accurate it's probably the messy spectacle of who I was back then, and the necessarily painful journey to the person I am now, for which I apologize. You shouldn't have to witness it, but try as I might – and trust me, I tried everything short of lawsuits and suicide – I find it impossible to tell Ethan's gloriously troubled story any other way.

1995. God, this hateful manuscript has taken that long to finally find its way to the publisher. As I write these last honest words for the opening pages – words I could have never written when I actually began the book – I remember that it was snowing in New York City when Ethan sailed his boat away from the United States, a strong and resilient man who'd been badly beaten and very nearly broken. I thought we were close back then, but over the years that I've tortured myself because of this manuscript I've learned there was so much about him I didn't know, and even more I didn't know about myself.

It was on that comfortably chilly 27th that the post office delivered a cardboard box to my office in the city, the address in Ethan's handwriting but the box too large to be one of his manuscripts. After sitting at my desk and pondering it for several minutes, I finally assumed that the box contained a gift, and I was excited because I didn't get many gifts. I could give you lots of good reasons for that and possibly even convince you of their validity, but the brutal truth I now know is that I just didn't deserve them. Life is sometimes as simple as that.

At that time I'd been Ethan's literary agent for more than a decade, and over those years I'd sent him a few books and videos, but no real gifts and certainly nothing personal because that wouldn't have been professional. Back then I *acted* friendly to everyone I worked with, but always found it best to keep a safe distance. Writers, you see, always wanted more from me than I could afford to give, and editors could at any time hurt my career more than I could endure. So I quite proudly kept people at arm's length. But somehow, from the very moment we met on the dais at a writer's conference, Ethan made me feel that I could trust him, so perhaps I did on occasion get too personal. If so (and at these closing moments I won't even bother to deny it), I regret none of it.

I remember smiling as I tore into the package, a child's smile, it seems, full of hopeful expectation and – hard for me to look back and believe – even innocence. A smile made memorable by the long and almost painful stretch it caused in my cheeks, yet linked to a reason too long past to recall exactly. I did try because I thought it might be important, but eventually chalked my rare flash of happiness up to nothing more significant than my closing a book deal that morning, or reading a promising new writer among the graduate school clones or last-gasp seniors, both of whom tended to "write what they knew" by memorializing their lives, the young in dark vignettes and the old in tedious memoirs. Or maybe I'd actually found a unique new voice among the unstructured amateurs whose pitch letters proclaimed that "My friends all love my writing and this is sure to be a best-seller." I didn't have many reasons to smile back then, so the range of options was narrow.

Inside Ethan's carton and carefully wrapped was a weathered wooden box about ten by fourteen inches, and five inches tall. It was made of oak and wonderfully crafted, probably a hundred years old and maybe twice that or more. Blotches of colors and smears of graphite seemed to testify that an artist, or perhaps a long legacy of artists, had carried paints, pencils, and brushes in it. They'd used it well over the years, and so I had no doubt at all as to why Ethan bought it. He needed, and perhaps it was a weakness, to keep things like that among artists, "even gutless writers" as he often panned himself "so that the inspirations of its former owners might have a decent chance at being passed along." It's funny to think of him that way now, but after a little too much wine and the accompanying slide from the tough guy persona he'd perfected through so many years of trading in unspeakable violence, that's exactly the kind of thing he would say.

I didn't allow myself to open the box for more than a minute, taking time to admire its exterior and imagining Ethan scouring dusty antique stores to find it. The latch was of a clever yet functional design. Silver plates protected the corners, and the dark smudges of carrying hands wrapped around the bottom and part way up the sides. I loved it, but as soon as I opened it any thoughts the box was a gift vanished. Even all this time that's passed has done nothing to dim my amazement over the box's contents, secrets I would never share if they'd belonged to me. Ethan had filled the box, probably over the span of several years, with personal keepsakes and intimate letters that completely exposed him as a passionately devoted man. And devoted to what? To a woman he loved, of course, but certainly not a woman who seemed to love him back.

The box was a wound. It was deep and fatal and festering with pain over that confused and sick woman who tortured this beautiful man and then left him for another. At least that's the way I saw it then, and although I've since been able to see some of the tremendous joy they shared so powerfully, there are still streaks of truth in that now blurry image.

I was soon to learn that Ethan had spent his last day in America absolutely alone, making notes on the photos and letters I held in my lap before writing an accompanying one to me. In it he explained his reasons, none of them valid, for abandoning everyone who loved him to live alone on his boat, sentencing himself to drift around the Caribbean and South America, making ports in places I'd heard him mention before, but only in passing.

The box also contained dozens of letters from the woman he loved – some of them wonderfully sweet, many others scrawled tearfully in the grip of anxiety or the well of depression – as well as photographs and keepsakes from a relationship that burned more feverishly than a junkie's addiction for all of those years, and is, I'm now sure, still smoldering and very much alive, hardened and purified into its final precious form by the enormous pressures against it.

I stayed in my office that entire night as I would never have been able to sleep anyway. I couldn't stop reading the letters and cards or staring at the photographs, finding the answers I'd always sought about the past Ethan kept such a secret, as well as hurtful insight into his life with this woman. I found myself attaching meaning to the trinkets they cherished, and squeezing significance from the hundreds of pictures of them together. Whether taken in 1986 or 1995 or any year in-between, nearly every photo captured them in a moment of undeniable happiness and unbreakable unity. He is always holding her close and she always has the arms of her tiny body wrapped tightly around him as if hanging onto something she loves as deeply as she needs.

I was so thankful for the photos, and could never have written this book without them because I needed their reassurance when strained or pleading letters spoke of the impossible challenges of their relationship, making me so skeptical I often thought their love was a lie they'd told themselves, and then convinced everyone around them to believe. But whenever I felt that way those photos – just one quick glance into the eyes of two people who loved each other so recklessly – proved how wrong I was.

As you'll learn in the pages that follow, I was several months into this project before I saw through the national legend that swirled and grew around Ethan and this woman as only a modern media frenzy can do. What I finally discovered was that although they seemed destined to canonization as one of the great romantic couples of our times, theirs wasn't anything close to a perfect love. Almost everyone I interviewed admired and envied them, but also knew their relationship was far from ideal, very difficult, and at times, impossible. What made it beautiful and rare was that through their amazing intimacy and her devastating sickness the two of them were unquestionably in love. It would be terribly difficult not to admire something that rare, and perhaps that alone makes this a story worth telling, the way it always has.

I confess that I didn't want to write this book for a very simple reason: At that time in my life I was probably the least likely person in New York to capture in words the incredible bond and devotion I gradually discovered between these two. I wasn't sure an attempt like that could ever be possible, but in their case it was even harder because so many of their letters were about difficult times they preferred to work through on paper, while dozens of cards and hundreds of photos showed they were too busy enjoying those great times to write about them.

What I found most compelling – incredible, really – was that as I did the research necessary to write *Loving Zelda*, I never once got the sense they ever thought they had hard times. Whether things were going great or terribly it was never *hard* because they always wanted to be with each other. They always had an absolute belief and expectation that things were going to work out and they would eventually find peace together. "Hard times," Ethan scribbled somewhere on the back of a photo, "are the ones that urge people to quit, to move on to some new partner who might be easier on the soul. That never happened to us. Even when we split up for ten months once, we never quit wanting each other, never gave up on our dream elusive. I'm sure we never will."

At this point I feel obligated to make my second confession – God, I feel like I'm back in therapy: "Hi, I'm Molly and I confess to being here at gunpoint" – and admit that I'd never worked on a love story before *Loving Zelda,* and to apologize for finding myself the unlikely narrator of this one. Writing about love, whatever the hell that might mean to me or you or the couple ignoring each other at the next table, is not a topic that usually interests me. Even when Ethan would craft a nicely written love scene in a thriller he was writing I would cringe and write "yuck" in the margin, insulting him in a way I didn't understand at the time. Only after opening the box did I discover how highly developed his sense of love was, so either I wasn't paying attention all those years of being his agent or I wasn't capable of understanding. For the person I was back then, those love scenes were as out of place in his thrillers as they were in the hectic pace of my life, although I deeply regret that now.

From the first words I ever read of Ethan's, his writing has intrigued me, whether they were e-mails, notes, or silly dedications from book signings: quick but thoughtful scribblings that always hinted at some kind of friendship with the book buyer. Ethan always took time to make everyone feel they were friends, and at first I thought it was just smart marketing, the way a salesman might cajole a receptionist. But I eventually came to understand that he needed their friendships, as if trying to tame some insecurity deeply rooted in the family's constant moving during his youth. Sometimes at a major signing like BookExpo I'd urge him to hurry before people got tired of waiting in line, but he never listened. He would spend half a minute talking and kidding with the buyer in front of him until he learned something he could use to write a personal note.

I remember one woman named Edna who had to be forty years older than Ethan, buying his latest book for John, her husband. Ethan asked, "Does John have a sense of humor?" Edna, poised and dignified, her white hair perfectly in place, said he was an incurable practical joker, so Ethan wrote in the book: *Dear John, Edna and I had a wonderful evening. Her company is delightful, all the more so after a few drinks (I'm sure you know that). I want to thank you for trusting her with me.*

Oh, yeah, John, I hope you enjoy the book. Beats a t-shirt. Ethan Ross.

Edna blushed and grinned and looked like she could have skipped away. She showed the inscription to her friend and the two of them giggled like a couple of schoolgirls, looking back and, I swear to you, flirting with Ethan.

He could have that kind of wonderful, disarming effect on the people who nervously came to meet the hard and much tested "shooter" for the United States Government, a man who thinly fictionalized his own career into big-arena thrillers. I told him often how much fun he was to work with, and how much I liked his writing, and that I saved all of it. So I guess that's why he sent the box to me.

Over the ten years since Ethan sailed away we've written and e-mailed back and forth as we worked on new books and movie projects. Occasionally (and in my mind I saw these events taking place at lonely anchorages with no other people for hundreds of miles) he would slip into hopeful melancholy and write about his enduring love for this woman who hurt him terribly, and his own mistakes he would always hope to undo. They were wonderfully sad writings that accepted his situation yet never abandoned the dream that they'd be together again, making those letters among the most inspired and honest things I ever got a chance to read. They made me grieve for Ethan, even more than they made me want to track him down and force him to understand that it was over between them and long past time for him to move on – although I had no reason to believe in my ability to make that clear to him.

The genesis of this book was the contents of the box I received so many years ago. Either directly or indirectly, the pages that follow chronicle Ethan's story, based on his request that I organize his letters and messages into some logical sequence. My intimacy with this project has unfortunately included me in the vaguest elements of a plot line, and while I never would have dreamed I'd include my own painful epiphany in this telling, not only does it now seem to make sense, it also seems essential and honest. In order to write their complicated story of loss I had to understand it, and to understand it required me to take incredible risks. To keep my personal experience secret would have cheated both him and you, so I'm taking a deep breath as I expose to you the emotional corset in which I'd chosen to live. The selflessness of this writing is the hardest and best thing I've ever done, but through the terror and tears of my own honesty – an honesty I'm quite sure will make you hate me – I hope to shine their devotion onto you. Love is like a mirror, Ethan wrote in one of his books years ago. All it can do is reflect the love you show. Your choice; it's always your choice. Reflecting Ethan's bold love required a similar courage from me, so please – and I've never pleaded before in my life – judge me gently as you read.

Ethan's reckless and violent life, which I think most people would agree was self-destructive, always reminded me of Ernest Hemingway's, a writer adventurous who either disguised or expunged his past in his stories. But Ethan's favorite author was actually F. Scott Fitzgerald.

12

He loved Fitzgerald's writing while at the same time admired the intense and difficult love between him and his wife, Zelda. I vaguely remember a long ago e-mail where Ethan wrote, "This day some years back Fitz lost his great and true love to a fire at the asylum. Who could write after that, and why would he bother?"

I never understood that the two writers were tortured by the same un-winnable challenge until I read Ethan's letters in the box. He signed many of them Scotty or Fitz, and the more I learned about his own love the more I understood the significance. I think I'm safe in believing it was Ethan who nicknamed his partially crazy and totally wonderful lover Zelda, and so it seems appropriate to use that name for her as I write. I think both of them would like it.

As anyone who follows the news is no doubt aware, six months before the date of this writing Ethan sailed out of Nassau, Bahamas and into the teeth of a Category Four hurricane. I got an email just before he left that said the weather was worsening and not to worry, that only a fool would venture out into those seas. I called the dock master as soon as they fixed the phone lines and learned that despite his promise to stay in port, Ethan left shortly after writing me. I haven't heard from him since, and his boat, *Waiting*, hasn't shown up yet in any marina I've checked. But I like to think he's still alive.

Ethan's life is, or was, a quest for true love and a conscious rejection of all that's accepted so easily in its place. Finding that kind of love was something he had to have, a safe center in his erratic life, almost like the calm eye of a lethal hurricane. While most people seem content to settle for anything that comes close, Ethan never had a moment's doubt that perfect love was possible. Even if it escaped him in the end – and at this point I'd be the last person on earth to say it did – he saw the years he and Zelda not only survived, but often flourished against incredible odds, as absolute proof of its existence.

While working on this story, I've witnessed the amazing way their tragic yet inspired love touched dozens of their friends, and even people who met them only once. I think those people admired Ethan and Zelda because they needed a reason to continue their own faith in each other, and a more inspirational couple would be hard to find, perhaps even impossible.

Ethan would be proud to know that after all I've learned, I consider him an utter fool for love.

Perhaps we should all be so lucky.

*****

After the editor hired me to ghostwrite this story, I found myself miserably confused over how to best show the intensity, understanding, and passion the publisher wanted its readers to feel. Over the course of those months – and with lots of unappreciated interferences – I grudgingly began to understand that Ethan and Zelda came close, painfully close, to sharing life's most amazing experience, and just like spirituality, peace, or happiness, love was impossible to either see or prove.

That created the dilemma that eventually led to this unusual telling: How could I even attempt to show something so mystical? The best evidence I could hope to provide was the effect it had on the two of them, but I couldn't use either one as proof. I had the letters, sure, but I barely knew Zelda. And Ethan, God, he was far too secretive about himself. Although he was constantly making small talk and jokes, he'd spent his life using casual words to build a wall to hide behind, convincing people that he'd said everything on his mind when quite the opposite was true. On the few occasions when that didn't work and someone kept pressing him for details, he totally avoided self-exposure with a line that's been famous among his friends for years: "Sorry, but it's not my story to tell." Even if it clearly *was* his story.

This book became my crash course in the unfortunate ways that kind of self-protection and fear can conspire to make love impossible. I learned more working on this project than I have in twenty-seven years of denial and enumerable tries at therapy. Maybe it was nothing more than lucky timing, or because I was given no choice but to learn – the pressure to write requiring me to examine things I would normally choose to overlook.

Or maybe, just maybe, Ethan and Zelda gave me an unseen helping hand, an emotional crib sheet of what they'd learned through such a difficult relationship. I don't know, really, but as you'll discover in your reading I'm far different now from the person who wrote the next chapter – what was originally, in a much different form, the opening chapter for this book. I've finally managed to understand Ethan and Zelda's love for myself, and have reluctantly decided that the only way I could show it to you was through their effect on me. That required me to expose the bitter way I lived at the very beginning of this project that's now, thank God, at an end. It's shameful, sad, and perhaps even interesting to see how unhappy I was, especially since I didn't even realize it.

As I'm sure you can imagine, I'm nervous as hell about this. But here goes.

Molly Edwards – New York, NY
January 21, 2006

CHAPTER 2 - Where I Began

No one who knows me would be surprised that the clothes in my closet are almost uniformly gray or black, and that I always choose from this bland wardrobe according to whom I expect to meet each day. If it's someone desperate for my help I might dress casually, sometimes even wearing a loose dress and flats, although always something conservative that wouldn't send the wrong signal. New York is and has always been a professional city, and I've been proud to be one of the people who help make it that way, respected if not loved as a literary agent. No way could I be confused with those who come naively because of a movie they saw or an image they had in their mind. New York's a much nicer place than ever before, but it will always be tough. I've watched scores of young corporate acolytes leave in ruin or tears or both. They had no business here in the first place, so it was probably best.

I've made New York my home, the place I earn a good living. I not only survive here, I excel. There aren't many single women who can say that.

Looking back, I remember that on that particular day of such great importance I chose a severe and powerful black suit. My meeting was at nine and so I decided not to have coffee until afterward because the lower I spoke, the calmer and in-control I felt, and the more in command I appeared, the better my chances of winning. Rudy had always been nice to me and would help if he could, so the suit was probably overkill. But as in all other areas of my life, I saw no sense in running risks.

Rudy Needham was the publisher's senior editor, the man who purchased *Loving Zelda* and gambled big on it. He'd been around a long time and edited dozens of best sellers, as well as three Pulitzer Prize winners and a Nobel he called "A kiss of death. The Nobel made readers assume the work was too lofty for them." He'd purchased more books by my authors than any other editor. Nice guy or not, he was no one to trifle with.

I arrived at their building early, cleared security, and got on the elevator. Another of their writers must have been coming in that day because I rode up with a caterer and his cart of fruit, coffee, and pastries. With him was a media rep who plowed through pages of notes as if something might be missing from the one page recap he had on top, his client's daily schedule of appearances.

The caterer smiled but I was too concerned about something splashing onto my clothes, and wishing they'd merely given Ethan a catered meeting last time he was here on his only return to the States, a two-day trip from the islands. Instead, after our meeting, several editors and staffers took him and me to a late lunch that lasted all afternoon, and several of us made a night of it drinking in Tribeca.

As I think about it, that probably set the stage for all the interest those editors later had in this book about his love letters. I was promoting him only as a thriller writer back then, building on the success of his early books, but he was intriguing the publishing staff with his Southern manners and his goal of writing books that moved away from the violence of his past and made people feel more than fear or anger.

"Ethan has done all the things he writes about," I said to the table at large, trying to lay the groundwork for his next book about spies and counter-espionage. "Urban assault, tactical weapons, survival ... what's the one you say is like a knife fight in a phone booth?"

He looked bored or embarrassed by what I was saying. *Hey*, I remember thinking, *I'm working for you here.*"

"Close-quarter battle," he said, and then added quietly, "Not exactly the kind of thing you'd want etched on your tombstone."

"But fascinating to people who haven't done it," I said, trying to remind him that although he might want to move on to some new and gentler genre, thrillers were where I'd been able to sell him. Now wasn't the time to change.

"Ethan," interrupted one of the editors, and I was glad to have piqued her interest. "There's a love story in most of your books, and in some it's pretty intense. But you don't write many sex scenes. Why is that?"

What was it about love and sex that so preoccupied everyone? I personally found it tiresome that every manuscript I picked up seemed to include both love and sex as though they were obligatory scenes. It was my most constant source of frustration as I worked with my authors, and so at that moment – although I figured him too much of a gentleman to do this – I worried that Ethan might slam me for my determination to chase those scenes out of his books.

"I do write them," he said, and that sounded like he really might blame their omission on me. "But when I read them they seem limiting. They confine the scene to what's written rather than opening it to what the reader might imagine. I try not to restrict the lurid or sensitive extremes readers will go to on their own."

"Which are you, Ethan, lurid or sensitive?"

"Sensitive," he answered instantly. Then he flashed that great smile of his. "I have my share of lurid moments, to be sure, but overall I'm sensitive."

"For instance. A recent example."

Another round of drinks arrived and the woman took one, although she should have been drinking water instead, like me. Everyone toasted her question, including Ethan, who knocked back his Jack Daniels and said, "Sure, that's easy. My girl and I were supposed to go to a party one night, but she was exhausted from helping a friend through a crisis so we decided to stay at my house instead, which sits on several acres of heavy woods. It was a chilly night, at least for Florida. I made a light dinner, opened some wine, and moved us out to the back deck. I built a hot fire in my cast iron chimnea and after we ate we sat huddled in front of the fire, with darkness all around.

"Twenty minutes later it began to rain and Zelda started to go in. 'Wait,' I said, then grabbed two large umbrellas from the house, and braced them up to keep us dry. "I kept throwing wood into the fire, and at midnight we were still there caressing each other with voices we could never have duplicated without the heated air, the cool wine, and the cold rain pattering on stretched fabric overhead."

Yes, thinking back, it was probably Ethan telling that story that fertilized the egg of the monster that forced me to Rudy's office that day. Who could have guessed that such a short and simple anecdote would drag me such an impossibly long way along the road of my life?

I got off at the eighteenth floor and the receptionist nodded a greeting. He'd been there a year or two, working the desk and opening mail and helping wherever he could as he tried to learn the business. I didn't know his name, because he never wore a nametag.

"I'm here for my appointment with Rudy Needham." I didn't waste his time or mine with chitchat or insincere pleasantries. I wasn't one of those agents who sucked up to subordinates at publishing houses because of the help they might provide in gaining access to an editor.

"Mr. Needham is sick and won't be in today, Miss Edwards. I tried to call you."

I didn't say anything, just glanced at my cell phone and made the look significant.

"Your home. I called your apartment first thing but no one answered. Not even a machine."

"I unplugged it last night so I could work."

"Would you like to talk to someone else?"

"Is Patricia here? She's working on this too."

"Of course. Sixth door down on the left."

"I know."

He picked up his phone and punched three numbers. I heard my name as I walked away.

Patricia, young and nice and easy for even me to like, had been the first reader of the pitch for *Loving Zelda*. She was a good associate editor who preferred to communicate with agents and writers at arms length whenever possible, working through snail mail and e-mail but very little face to face. I understood that approach well, and was sure she appreciated me for it.

"Molly," she said as she greeted me at the door. "Come in. Hang on while I move this pile … no, tell you what, we'll sit over here on the couch. Less to shovel out of the way."

Her office could have been any editor's, or most agents' for that matter: stacks of clipped together papers sat on every flat surface, along with piles of unopened manila envelopes stuffed full of submissions. Cover flats and galleys were scattered everywhere, and her chair behind the desk was the only one regularly used for sitting.

She slid everything to the middle of the couch. "So, Molly, tell me what you've done on *Loving Zelda*. God, the ending of their story is so amazing. I bet that part is easy, but have you nailed the opening yet?"

She sat down at one end of the couch. I wished she'd kept standing because I was at least three inches taller, but once she sat I pretty much had to. I pulled the first chapter out of my briefcase and looked over the pages before handing them to her.

"I've been working on the angle of beginning with the letter Zelda's father wrote, the one where he talks about them chasing each other around in the party store while an old woman watched. It does a nice job of capturing the fun part of their relationship."

"I've got to tell you that I'm thrilled to be talking with you about this. It's such an exciting project for us. I mean, wouldn't everyone want to be loved the way they loved each other? Even if they did have a few problems? Heck, I have at least that much trouble with the guys I date and don't get anything close to their kind of love in return. I mean, for God's sake, he *never* stopped loving her. Never. It's … well, it's almost impossible for me to imagine, yet I believe it absolutely."

Her voice softened and she looked away with a drifty expression on her face. *Come on, Pat, snap out of it.*

I cleared my throat and she finally came out of her little-girl lovey-trance. "I'm not so sure about this opening scene though. I wrote it as a nod to lonely people, thinking it would resonate with so many readers who are looking in vain for love, pretty much what you were just talking about. But it felt too –"

"Revealing?" She looked way into my eyes and leaned across the couch toward me.

I couldn't stop myself from jerking away as if panicked. "Of course not," I said, forcing myself to lean again back in her direction. "Stupid. It felt stupid, not revealing."

I lowered the papers, and then put them back into my briefcase. "I'm sure it's the wrong place to start, Pat. It was ridiculous for me to attempt to write a scene that in truth I'd never want to see in print. And to be totally honest, it's more than just a bad start, because it infects everything that follows by moving the story in an unknown direction toward an unexpected ending that has the potential of disappointing the reader."

"My God, Molly, you can't possibly think their ending is disappointing."

"I think it could come off that way if not done right. This whole stupid story needs to be extremely well crafted if it's going to move the reader as emotionally as it should. To be honest, I'm not sure I can do it. All in all I'm thinking it might be better if you hired someone else, a more skilled writer."

"Really?"

"It is a great story. I know it's a great story – jeez, that's all I hear anymore – but expectations in the industry have grown so out of control that I'm wondering if I'm up to it, hell, if anyone's really up to it. I've already done a lot of work, research mostly, but I'm willing to hand it over and give back the entire advance because I don't want to risk a strain in our relationship."

"Molly, I was in the meeting when you begged for this."

"Beg is much too strong of a word, but yes, I did want to write it. I figured it would come natural to me but it doesn't. *LZ* is not the story Rudy thinks he bought and you seem to think I can write. He's expecting a story about a perfect love, not a relationship that crashed and burned so spectacularly."

"Don't sell us short, Molly. What Rudy bought – based on my recommendation I might add – was a romantic tragedy about two people battling overwhelming obstacles of sickness and ego and fear and uncertainty, standing against all that with such a heroic effort that even their failure, if that's what you ultimately decide, is still what Ethan originally said it was: a story worth telling. They loved each other, Molly, more than anything else. God damn it do you have any idea how rare that is? They never for an instant lost their determination to make it work on their own terms. Sit there and think about that for a moment."

"I have. You know I have."

"We're already three months into the schedule, with *Loving Zelda* scheduled for a pub date of January next to catch the following Valentine's Day. Maybe we could push it back if someone hadn't slipped the story to Hollywood when it was out on submission, but with them rushing the script and already into pre-production we have no choice but to get this book on the shelves as scheduled. We barely have enough time for *you* to write it, let alone start fresh with someone else."

"I'm sorry, but I'm just too close. There's no way I can see the whole story."

"If I remember correctly that's why you were given the job, and to be honest, why we paid you so much money to write it under Ethan's name. You've been close to him for twenty years. Jesus, you even met Zelda. You actually saw the two of them together!"

"I shouldn't have taken on a love story. Have you ever heard of me pitching one?"

"Never."

"That's what I mean. Come on, Pat, what about using Marek? He knows Ethan from other books they've worked on. They did a lot of brainstorming together on the structure for *The Boneyard*."

"Dick doesn't have the kind of history you do with Ethan. He's great, but you've got insight no one else has."

I stood and it surprised her, but she stayed seated.

"What if I just can't do it? Friend to friend, Pat, how much would it hurt me here?"

She rose slowly off the couch. I turned away, hoping she'd interpret it as pain or fear and therefore offer compassion.

I heard her walk up behind me. I was ready for her to touch me, to ask what's wrong, to wonder why it was so hard for me.

When she didn't stop I turned and saw that she'd gone back to her desk. She sat down, put on her glasses, and read whatever she was working on before I arrived. Then she looked up.

"Molly, if you screw us on this there'll be enough pain to go around you twice. And on a personal note I'll tell you this: Rudy is my friend. Jam him and I'll make sure nothing else you submit is ever read by us or any of our imprints. My mission. Got it? Great. Good-bye."

I was dumbfounded as I watched her scritch through a manuscript with a blue pen. The paper ripped and she looked up at me again. I decided it was best to leave.

As I signed out I wondered how damaging it would be if she carried out that threat, and how important one publishing house was to my business anyway. There could be another merger that would shake things up and crack open other possibilities, but did I really want to start burning bridges I'd worked so hard to build?

Come on, Molly. Just pull it together somehow. Write Ethan's damn book. You don't have to take the lid off your own box to expose what was in his. No one has to see you in this book. It's not even about you, so all you have to do is keep it that way.

But everything I wrote seemed to expose *me* as that "person as alone as she deserved to be," even in the little bits I'd struggled onto paper. Ethan's stupid letters had become a gnawing, infectious part of me. They'd destroyed any chance I ever had of objectivity.

MRS. BEECHAM followed them out of Target as they headed next door to the party store, a fun place full of great costumes and gag gifts and "Look Who's Over the Hill" yard signs. He was pushing forty and she was younger, followed by a set of parents and four pretty girls stacked close in the ages between five and ten.

The way the couple walked together and touched each other left no doubt in her heart, that they were from her tribe: an unfortunately rare breed who knew how great it was to be loved entirely by the person they entirely loved.

If love could be related to sleep – what a silly idea, but if it could – these two were in R.E.M. They had totally surrendered their fears and anxieties. They were completely vulnerable and receptive to each other.

So few like them around these days, she thought, but maybe they'd always been rare. She and Eddie had been, that's for sure. They'd heard it for sixty-one amazing years, the question usually phrased in kidding dialogue or jealous looks from people as alone as they deserved to be: What *is* it about you two?

The party store was Mrs. Beecham's favorite place, particularly in the days before Halloween when the manager let her sit on a stool behind the counter, keeping her safe from the festive madness but right where she could enjoy all of the fun and excitement of people being silly.

"Morning, Mrs. Beecham," said the young clerk by the door.

"Morning, Alyssa."

She normally asked about Alyssa's boyfriend, and Alyssa would wander the aisles talking as if Mrs. Beecham understood her feelings better than her friends or parents. But not today.

"That way, Mrs. Beecham."

"Pardon me, dear."

"I saw them too. They went down aisle four."

Mrs. Beecham hobbled back and gave her a hug, then squeezed her hands. "So exciting to see, isn't it dear?"

"Beautiful."

"This is that rare thing I've been describing for months. Do you and Dustin have anything close to what those two have?"

"No, ma'am, we don't."

"Then don't settle, dear. Never settle."

"Now that I've actually seen it, I won't. I promise."

"Good for you." Then Mrs. Beecham winked and pulled Alyssa along. "Come on. Let's see what they're up to."

"I'm with you."

They heard the laughter before they got to the aisle, a range of loving voices that made both women smile.

"Hurry, dear. What do you think they're doing?"

"Sounds like ... watch out, Mrs. Beecham."

The man suddenly ran out from the aisle with the woman on his heels like a couple of children on a playground. He was laughing and holding his side as she chased after him and the rest of the family followed. The parents – Mrs. Beecham could tell they were her parents – had to stop because they were laughing too hard. The daughters split up and shouted encouragement and directions.

"Dad, look out, she's going down the other aisle."

"Get him, Mom. Tickle him back."

The tiny woman shouted "Pardon me" as she ran around Mrs. Beecham and Alyssa.

"Wait," said Mrs. Beecham. "In the mirror, dear. Look, there he is!"

The little woman stopped running, and all three of them looked up and saw the reflection of him crouching near the end of the next aisle, a grown man playing tag in a store.

"It's Ethan," squealed the woman. "I've got him now. Thanks."

"Tickle him for me," giggled Mrs. Beecham. Then she turned and jabbed Alyssa in the ribs and made her jump. "Sorry, dear, couldn't help myself."

The man ran out the door. The woman who loved him was catching up, although it looked like he might actually be letting her. The four girls cheered their favorites as they and the parents poured out of the store like a March wind passing, full of all the good things a winter world craved. Mrs. Beecham couldn't resist the temptation of going after them.

CHAPTER 3 - Part of the Letter Ethan Wrote to Accompany the Box

Dear Molly,

You've heard nothing from me as I've struggled through a very bleak time in my life. Sorry to have shut you out as I made some tough decisions over which I'm sure we would have argued. I'll tell you about them in a minute.

The box in front of you is where I've stored my most precious memories of a woman I've just recently lost. I've spent all afternoon and evening making notes on the letters and pictures and poems that might touch you somehow, hoping you'll see something worthwhile as I try to connect the letters to the experience and fill in what's missing, clues to help you understand why my loss is so painful, and perhaps help you avoid similar pain in your own life. This story is so personal that it's difficult to tell, yet at the same time I know it will be oddly familiar to almost everyone.

Molly, you're a smart lady and an excellent agent who has always dreamed of writing your own book. I think you should, so this is my contribution, my effort to motivate you to the dream you have not yet begun to chase. I know a love story would be your last choice, but it's all I can do. The worlds I know well and have written about so extensively are too covert, intricate, and training-intensive for me to pass on anything you could turn into a book. But in a world where emotions are universal, my life with Zelda seems unique. I believe that it's truly a story worth telling, so perhaps among these scraps and scribbles that mean so incredibly much to me you'll find the inspiration you need. Maybe someday, just for an interesting reversal of roles, I'll be reading your novel. How proud of you I'll be.

What follows is the first thing I ever wrote about Zelda, a fictional little fantasy for her alone, born of the belief I'd never have her in my life, how I imagined struggling through without her, and my dream of her eventually coming to find me. Of course, we did end up together after the story was written, but it's interesting that from the perspective of so many years' distance, the story still seems prophetic. When I tell you what I'm about to do, you'll think I should have made a career of predictions instead of writing. Have I been living a life that's a self-fulfilled prophesy, or did I quite accurately predict the life I was destined to live? It's an interesting question, and one I'll have lots of time to ponder. – Ethan

I WAITED TWO years after discovering what love actually felt like before telling the woman I loved her. Her name is Zelda, and to my eyes and my heart she is the most beautiful woman I have ever known. She smiles so quickly it astounds me, and when she looks into my eyes I forget everything but her, leaving me un-motivated to survive without her, even as I'm tortured in her presence. I ache constantly for her touch, for her smell, for the thrill of being close to her.

I should never have told her I loved her, because once those dangerous words slipped over my lips, our lives changed forever. Our love was too strong, our affection too pure, our devotion too perfect. We could not control our own hearts and they instantly belonged to each other, although she was married and unwilling to leave her husband, at least back then. I had no way of knowing that her marriage was just the first of many things that would keep us apart.

That following summer, the articles I'd been writing for years started to sell. Soon after that, a book I'd ghostwritten became a bestseller, and I suddenly had the freedom to work anywhere, earning enough to provide for my children as they finished school and moved toward college and great futures of their own.

I named the 46' sailboat I now live aboard *Waiting*, and sailed to the Caribbean to live alone and write. The morning before I left, I met Zelda for the last time and gave her a short story I'd written about the two of us, along with an envelope with my agent's phone number and some cash. Get-away money, I'd called it. Come-find-me-whenever-you're-ready money.

Since then, I've lived an isolated life in the islands. No one has taken Zelda's place in my heart or my life as I live alone on *Waiting* and communicate with the States through faxes and letters. Three weeks ago the news I anticipated all these years arrived – an envelope from my agent that contained Zelda's letter. Would I meet her, it asked, in St. Thomas? She would be there sometime on March 18, would check the marinas for my boat, but would understand if I stayed away.

So here I sit in the cockpit of *Waiting*, writing these few lines as I search the pier for Zelda. I've had islanders cleaning the boat since I arrived from Tobago four days ago, but I have just sent them away with my sincere thanks and too much money.

I wait and write and look out at the boats in the harbor straining against their moorings. Each one of them is alone and separated, as I have been so long, so I begin to wonder about Zelda's heart and start to worry. Is it still mine? Will she ever be mine?

Then a voice from the dock calls my name. It is the voice that eases me to sleep every night and wakes me every morning and haunts every moment that lives in between. I look slowly, afraid that her husband will be beside her, or that her eyes will tell me a sad, new truth, or that her lips will not look like they want to kiss me.

Those fears evaporate like bad dreams when the lights go on. She is alone and smiling. Her eyes set off the wild animal who lives caged in my chest, and I climb clumsily onto the dock. I catch her scent as I step close. Then I step again, locking her into my eyes and my memory. But I do not dare touch her. It feels far beyond any privilege I can ever imagine.

I stand inches away, weak and waiting, until she raises her arms and drapes them around my neck, pulls me close and kisses me. Our bodies tangle together. My arms pull her so tightly she gasps. I will never let go of her again.

*****

Molly, a few months ago you sent me an advance copy of Keyes' wonderful new book, *The Courage to Write*, and urged me to read it because you wanted more honesty from me in my writing. He struck a nerve, I admit, so here's a healthy dose of *Honest Ethan* for you: I am right now sitting on the floor of my empty home and want desperately to cry over what I've lost, and all I've decided to leave behind, and my own ego and stupidity for making the former happen and the latter necessary, leaving me few other choices but this terribly sad journey on which I'm embarking. That brings me to the odd news I promised.

I've sold this home I love so much and gave away anything my friends or kids wanted. I gave the buyers a great deal because I couldn't bring myself to either tear it down or finish the remodeling I'd started in anticipation of Zelda moving in with her two daughters. I remember being a little boy watching John Wayne torch a room for similar reasons in a rerun of *The Man Who Shot Liberty Valance*, and that's exactly what I wanted to do – set the whole damn thing on fire. Leaving the remodeling unfinished was the next best thing, I guess.

I had a closet that was crammed full of business clothes I seldom wore and the tuxedo I dusted off for the Edgar Awards each year. I gave all that to Goodwill because I have very little room on the 40' sailboat I purchased and named *Waiting*, just like in the fictional story.

I had another closet that was empty save for a dark blue dress with small white dots. It's not really a long dress, but it hung long on the tiny woman who wore it the night I told her I loved her. That was nine years ago. It somehow feels like a day and my entire life at the same time.

Last week, after the forces that Zelda and I battled for years finally overwhelmed us, that dress was the one thing I asked from her. I wanted to remember the instant our relationship began rather than the way it ended. When she brought it by my house she also returned nine years worth of letters I'd written her, the ones you see in front of you.

Her new fiancé, Mike, waited in the car as she stood on my porch and asked, "Can I have your dog tags?" Her eyes cut to his car, and I knew she just wanted something small of mine, something readily available that she could conceal as she walked down the drive toward her new life.

"Sure," I said, as I leaned out of Mike's sight and took the chain off my neck. "I'll never stop loving you, Z. I'm positive you know that."

She was barely under control, surely afraid that saying anything would cause a breakdown, and I wanted to hate Mike for coming along and putting her in this stressful position between us. But he was too new to understand how quickly this beautiful, fragile woman could spiral into depression. I like to think he wouldn't have come along if he had known. In fact I'm sure he wouldn't have.

A car door opened and closed. Mike stood still for only a second before taking a few steps toward the house.

"I've got to go," she said, and then held out her hand. As I shook it I pressed my dog tags into her palm. It was the last time I would touch her and I paid absolute attention. I wanted to remember everything as I once again became Zelda's secret lover. I'd done it all those years when she was married to Paul, and I would be doing it now for as long as she was with Mike.

I love having that dress. Before packing it away I touched it to my face, felt the silky fabric slide against my skin, and remembered the excitement of putting my hands on its sheer shimmer while it hung on her tiny body. It was the very last thing I packed, just a few hours ago, folding it tightly before putting it in a freezer bag and squeezing out the air that still, somehow, smelled of the perfume she wore.

Molly, as I walk around the large rooms and unfinished carpentry of this big house, it's interesting to realize how little I really need. All the tools, bikes, cars, and furniture I accumulated since my long-ago divorce are gone. The house is empty except for a couple of duffle bags, a small box of kitchen tools, and a cat.

I sit down on the floor beside Smudge, who is sure something's wrong. All her favorite places to hide or sleep are gone.

"You'll be fine, fleabag. The girls will take great care of you."

I scratch her head and she purrs. I'd like to take her with me but I also want to feel adrift, going anywhere and nowhere, the wind blowing me through my future as though I'm the Flying Dutchman of relationships. I don't want the challenge of a pet, and to be honest I don't want the company. It's self-indulgent, I'm sure, but I want to suffer alone.

"You know what really sucks, Smudge?"

She cocks her head so I'll scratch the other ear.

"It's that I only now realize how screwed I am. It's terrible to know what it's like to be truly loved by the person I love truly."

She doesn't get it, I can tell.

"You'd think that makes me unbelievably lucky, but it doesn't. It's cursed me. How can I ever settle for anything less now?"

She hears something outside and springs to the window.

"Don't bother answering," I say.

The truth, Molly, is that I can't.

– Ethan, February 20, 1995

CHAPTER 4 - The Phone Call, Almost Ten Years Later

"Zelda?" I said, thrown off a little by the loss of the accent I remembered from meeting her once in Florida. "*The* Zelda? You've got to be friggin' kidding me."

The name had never slipped into that hard to reach corner of my memory, and so even after all those years my gut reaction was to climb down the line and strangle the woman on the other end. Back then – long before I even thought about writing this book – I had no understanding of the emotional problems she had, or the challenges Ethan caused her, or the powerful magnetism that kept them so completely attracted through both those difficulties. All I felt at the time was that it would have been impossible for one person to ever hurt another more than she hurt Ethan.

I could hardly believe she actually had the nerve to call me. Furthermore I knew exactly why she'd called. She had finally gotten around looking for Ethan so she could screw up however much of him had managed to survive her last dose of punishment. Maybe this time she would hurt him enough to kill him.

"You remember my name after all this time, Molly? That's nice of you."

"I know who you are."

"The letter Ethan left behind said you would. Is he okay?"

What do you think? He's sad and alone and living for years like a castaway on some damned boat, and it's totally your fault.

"He's fine. Never better. Last I heard was that he'd met someone nice, a woman in Belize, I think."

"Really?"

I listened for pain but heard only confusion, as if she didn't know what to say next.

"I'm not really sure," I said after a few seconds. "A rumor."

"Well, I'm glad he's okay. I've been worried. Can you get a message to him?"

Sure, I'll give him a message that you wouldn't care if he fell off his boat and drowned, that you never loved him and never will, that the emotions you shared so long ago were just stupid and foolish, the kind that try to trap all of us at one time or another.

I stopped biting my lip and said "Yes."

She told me what she wanted me to do, and as I wrote down the information my pen shattered. Ink stained my fingers and ruined my blouse but I didn't say anything that might let her know. I'd always been able to hold anything in, to hold everything in. She would never know she'd upset me. No one ever did.

"Thank you," she said.

"You're very welcome."

I'm sure there were teeth marks in my tongue.

I didn't think I would ever understand how she could have been so cruel to such a nice man. Nor could I imagine what horrible new things she'd cooked up for him before calling me. But I'd promised Ethan long ago that if this day ever came I would do as he asked, and I tried hard to keep my promises, even if I hated what it required me to do. As impossible – *impossible* – as it was for me to understand, I knew he'd be happy to hear from her, so that was something, I guess.

I called the marina where *Waiting* had docked for several days and left a message for Ethan. He didn't call back, but I received this story by e-mail on December 6, 2004, about a week later. It was the next to the last thing I ever read of his, although I'll always hope to read more.

Hey Molly-Girl,

I haven't written anything of merit since I fell out of the rigging and broke my arm, a spectacular feat of acrobatics over which I still feel pretty stupid. I'm sure you know that your message brought me more excitement than I've had in years, so if you have any kind of bad news for me (an I.R.S. audit, the return of Prohibition, a Spice Girls reunion), send it now because I won't mind at all. I feel like I'm eighteen again, or drunk.

No, that's not right. What I feel is the same enthusiasm I used to get after a long time away, when I finally got orders for home. And I don't mean just home to America, but home to Zelda.

After exiling myself down here for so many lonely years, I'm on my way back, Molly. It's so hard to believe, but I never once lost faith in our love. I'm sure you always knew that. I'm equally sure you never understood.

Unfortunately, my sudden good fortune leaves in doubt for a bit longer when I'll get the final manuscript of the new thriller to you, so just to prove that the rope burns, boat drinks, and bumps on the noggin haven't totally destroyed me, I'll write down the events your phone call set in motion. Don't be too critical because it's just a quickie as I rush to get ready to see Zelda later today.

Thank you so much, Molly. You have no idea how happy you've made me. When I remember how to wear shoes and city clothes I promise you a big hug and a raucous night out back in New York! – Ethan

ALBERTO IS THE DOCK MASTER where I've tied up *Waiting* for several days. He's a small Tico with several cute kids who hang around his marina like faithful cats.

He raced his youngest boy down the finger pier toward my boat. I was stooped over the bow repairing the roller furling, but when I heard their sandals slapping the wood I stood up to watch. Not just because I needed to stretch (which I did), but because their pace was too fast for such a relaxed culture.

The warm breeze of a Costa Rican evening blew back their dark hair and kept their laughter from reaching my ears, but I could see them laughing and it made me smile. It took far too many years and an incredible woman for me to learn how to enjoy simple pleasures like laughter, but I've been doing it so long now that I'm nearly always smiling. I thank God daily for that.

"Mr. Ross," Alberto shouted as he stopped running and gave Mario the victory. "I have some news. A message."

"Buenos Dias, Big Al."

He blushed each time I called him that, but I'm sure he liked it because he always stood taller, like he was growing into a reputation. I stepped onto the dock and bent toward the boy. "You run fast, Mario. Will you run with me someday?"

"Not you, Senor Ross. I see you run all the time, fast and far."

"We'll make it an easy run, my friend. Let me know. I could use the company."

I shake Big Al's hand. "A message?"

"Yes. A woman called all the way from New York City. Your agent. She sounded sad, I'm afraid, but said this would make you happy. She is fond of you, I can tell."

Stringing the words *sad* and *happy* into the same sentence told me this was about Zelda, and that made me suddenly afraid of the news that could change my life again. I stared at Alberto, afraid to take my eyes off him because I didn't know what else to do, and at least staring at him was *something*. I smiled enough to hide my jitters, all the time wanting to sit down on the dock or pace up and down or fidget my hands around in the air. I wanted to ask Alberto why he hadn't come down the pier and gotten me instead of taking a message, worried about how much might have been lost to the nuances of languages,

43

but sure that even a terrible interpretation would still convey the meaning.

"I know she cares," I said softly, still on his eyes as I straightened myself into my best posture since the day I sailed away from Florida nearly a decade ago. "So, good news, huh? That's always nice." I reached over and fiddled with the roller furling, hoping to look unaffected by Alberto, and immediately pinched my finger in the mechanism. I pulled my hand away and stood there stupidly as blood dribbled away.

Alberto gently lifted my hand and nodded to Mario, who chased off down the pier for a first aid kit, I suppose. I didn't care.

"A woman named Zelda called her. She wants to see you again. She'll be in Nassau Friday of next week."

Alberto squeezed closed my cut and watched my eyes. He is a compassionate and patient man, and I was very glad for both virtues because at that moment I couldn't speak. The woman who broke my heart twice was coming to see me. What do you say to someone who tells you amazing news like that?

"Thanks," I said as I pulled my hand away from him, applied a little pressure, and climbed over the lifelines onto my boat. I had to concentrate to avoid falling into the water or tripping on a deck plate. "Thanks," I said again, as Alberto smiled at the way I was behaving. Then he said something that, loosely interpreted, meant "a blessing on your future."

I left within the hour and sailed *Waiting* single-handedly from Costa Rica. It was just my luck to get this news during hurricane season, with a good-sized one forming up in the Atlantic and forecasted to head my way. If it had been closer I would have had little choice but to stay put or hire an experienced crew, but I had plenty of time and was glad not to wait for better weather, or to have strangers onboard to muddle my thoughts. I could outrun the storm, sailing alone with my memories. I would ride out the hurricane in Nassau.

I made port two days ago. I immediately hired a local man and his wife to scrub and clean every bit of the boat, wash the towels and linens, polish the wood and bright work, replenish the wine and get rid of all symbols of a man living alone – as I'd done since Zelda and I broke up. Yesterday I went to a barber and then bought some new clothes, and when I returned to *Waiting* my short hair and clean-shaven face were all it took to make the giggles of my cleaning crew turn to laughter. I was scared and nervous as a young man meeting his first date and they found it funny. Hell, I would have found it funny too if I wasn't so damned terrified.

First thing this morning they came by again, this time with a basket of fruit and a flower. "Give her this when she steps aboard," said the woman as she handed me a huge island lily. "It will be good luck for you." Then she smiled, hugged me, and gave me a sisterly kiss. "The fruit is for later."

She left and I showered. I dressed and waited, sitting in the cockpit watching the last commercial jet make its final approach before the airport closed, and hoping that Zelda had already arrived. About three o'clock I went down to shower again because I was just a little ripe from my nerves and the Caribbean sun. The wind and waves from the oncoming hurricane rocked my boat hard, even in the harbor. Water slopped out of the shower and made a bit of a mess on the clean floor.

As you must know, Molly, when Zelda and I met twenty years ago we were given a rare gift, and shame on both of us for treating it carelessly, for letting so many things, including my massive ego, get in the way of us both having confidence in each other. More than any two people I've ever heard or read about, we were in love, and by that I mean the kind that inspires everyone who sees it. Ours wasn't like any love I'd experienced before and it didn't grow complacent with age. After nearly a decade together the sound of her voice or the touch of her skin were more powerful than the first time we talked, or the night I first held her on the dance floor. It was as if Zelda and I had captured a legend or proven the existence of God, it was that amazing, that rare, and that beautiful. We screwed it up, sure, but that doesn't mean it didn't exist or doesn't still.

I've heard people say that the intensity of a love like that can't last, that there's no way to sustain a relationship with that much passion. That wasn't the case for Zelda and me, so I know they're wrong. The intensity can last, so I think people who never find that kind of love have no choice but to say that for their own comfort. To believe otherwise would force them to see the shortfalls of the relationships they do have. They'd have no choice but to accept the fact they've settled, and no one wants to believe that.

The challenge about a love where the intensity builds rather than diminishes, at least as I see it, is that its rarity in the human experience gives us little chance to prepare for it. That's why we put it at risk by trying to make it even more perfect than it already is, believing somehow that perfect devotion should equal a perfect relationship. It's taken the last ten years of my life to learn that lesson, to take responsibility for my glimpse of something so rare making me want even more of it. Like a miner who savages the landscape he loves for the silver within, I destroyed the beauty that appeared so naturally and perfectly between Zelda and me by wanting even more of it.

That's all going to change today with a huge apology and a vow to accept her as she is, to never again try to change her at all. Any minute within the next few hours, my Zelda is going to walk down the pier and stand by my boat and call my name and it's going to be as if we never lost a minute. We separated for ten months once – it was the last time we broke up before she left me to marry Mike – but the instant we saw each other we went back to exactly where we'd left off. When the fit is perfect, it's always a perfect fit, even if the pieces have been separated for years, as ours has been.

I wonder if she's changed. Maybe she's gotten heavy. Maybe she's even sicker than she was before. Maybe she's been so hurt by Mike that she won't be happy. Maybe he abandoned her when she was desperate for help, and I wasn't there to help her either.

None of that matters. She is the woman I love, and certainly not for her health. Nor does my love depend on her being happy. If she's sad I'll cheer her up. If she's sick I'll care for her. I know better than anyone else does how to do that. If she's been hurt I'll promise it will never happen again, and enjoy as many years as it takes to prove it. If she's fat as an old housecat … I couldn't care less. I love her so much I'll probably never notice.

CHAPTER 5 - The Screenwriter

"He's still holding on line three, Molly."

Why won't he leave me alone? I sent him copies of everything in Ethan's box so that should put me out of it. I'm having enough troubles just writing the book. "Tell him I left."

"He said 'if she says she's left one more time I'll tell the producers she's not cooperating.' He's pretty frustrated."

"Okay, Heather, I'll take it."

Why am I straightening in my chair? Don't you dare let this guy bully you, Molly. "This is Molly Edwards."

"Hey, it's Frank. Hang on a minute."

Is he eating? Damn, he is eating. I have a million things to do and I'm listening to this guy chew food.

"Mr. Reynolds, I'm a little busy."

"Me, too, but I started my lunch while I was on hold for so long. Almost finished now."

"Stale bread and bologna? The diet of a struggling screenwriter?"

"Cute. Listen, I've started the screenplay of *Loving Zelda*. Fascinating story and I want to run the opening by you."

"I've only been hired to ghostwrite the book. Whatever you do with the movie is completely –"

"Just thought we might as well be on the same page, okay? Besides, I'm opening the movie with you, although I haven't picked your name yet."

He'll probably call me Bitsy or Sunny or something like that. It's what a man like him would do.

"I'd rather not be in the movie."

"Already ran it by the producers. They love the idea."

"Then I'll call you back when I have time to discuss it."

"Just take a few secs. I'm going to open with you in your office, typing the letter to yours truly that accompanied Ethan's box of goodies. You'll look pissed off and sad yet determined to move past it as you pick up the box, put in the letter, and close it. As you hold the box your hands will fade out, and on the other side of the box Ethan's hands will fade in. For a second you'll both be holding it, but something – I still got to figure this out – shows that ten long years have passed between the time he sent it to you and you sent it to me. Like it so far?"

I look at my watch. Of course, he can't <u>see</u> me look at my watch, so what's the point? "Sounds fine."

"Good. As your hands fade out the camera will pull away and elevate toward the ceiling, looking down like God as Ethan sits on the floor of his empty house surrounded by all of his Zelda treasures. It's his last night in America, right, and he's sold everything and bought the boat. He writes his note to you, and then collects the photos and puts them all in the box, the way you did in the previous scene I just described. He wraps it up and puts it in a cardboard box. Your address is on that. Maybe I can work the date in there. Not sure."

"You'll figure it out."

"Yeah. Anyway, I think that will work as an opening, particularly if there's some narration, maybe Ethan talking about the costs and pain of his love, or maybe a meaningful song. But that's about as far as I can go without your help because I come up short on the love story."

"That's all you've done?" *Maybe I can buy some time if the screenplay is late.*

"I did find time to clip my toenails and draft the scene where Ethan calls Zelda's husband after finding her drivers license. He takes it by their house while he's out riding his bicycle. Paul introduces him to Zelda and Boom! Everyone feels the passion. Ethan is sweaty from the ride and obviously uneasy in her gaze; Zelda's looking at the man she's always wanted but never knew; and poor Paul sees he's just met the man who'll eventually take away his wife. Good actors will convey all of that in little expressions, the smaller the better as everyone pretends to feel nothing."

"Okay."

"From there, well, I've read all the letters but there's too much missing. Hell, a bunch of the letters were about their problems. Not all, I know, but I can't write a love story about two people

51

who couldn't beat the odds against them being together."

"Shakespeare could. Ever read Romeo and Juliet?"

"That's a point. Is that how you see this story, how you're writing the book?"

"I'm still working it out, same as you."

"Even the old bard himself would need to know more."

"Then you really should be asking Jonathan for advice."

"Who?"

"Jonathan Green."

"Their friend the artist? I've heard of him."

"Most everyone who's truly in the arts has. In your case, I mentioned him in our last conversation."

"You just can't be nice."

"He seemed to understand their love better than anyone else. He wasn't just Ethan's or Zelda's friend because although he met them at the same time, he liked them both for entirely different reasons. I think Jonathan and Zelda were a lot alike in some ways."

"My wife hates my friends. Your husband hate yours?"

"I'm not married."

"Now. You're not married now, but I assume you *were* married, right? Did your husband hate your friends?"

I can just imagine this guy married, hating his wife, cheating and joking his way toward a divorce or a fight to the bitter end.

"I've never married. I work too hard."

"So I should've worked harder. I'll remember that next time."

Ah, yes, the joke, probably with bologna in his teeth.

"Just kidding. I love my wife."

"I'm sure you do."

"Jonathan painted the picture, right? The one his kids donated to the museum?"

"That's right. I sent you a litho."

"Pretty generous of the kids. Must be worth fifty grand or more, considering all the publicity surrounding the painting and Ethan and Zelda."

"I wouldn't know, Mr. Reynolds."

"That's the number, fifty grand. I called the lady in charge at the museum. Surprised?"

"You're amazing."

"So how about getting some details from Green. I can tell that Ethan and Zelda were nuts about each other, no doubt about it. Even I'm jealous of what they had together, but there's more to the story and I want to know it. You're earning big money because of their story. I know you won't get credit for the book, but you got a big commish for the movie and it's time to earn it."

He hung up, leaving me to wonder why the studio picked such an ass to write such a beautiful story.

I should have been able to focus myself around the guy, keeping my concentration on making new deals, but he was right about the sale of film rights. It was a major accomplishment, and perhaps more important than just the money I earned, I also hoped the movie would elevate me a few places on the list of top New York agents, attracting the best writers who would give me exclusive first looks at quality works that explored the edges and the extremes. That was the race I ran and the rabbit I chased, to the exclusion of everything else in life. A few pegs up the ladder could make the rabbit more likely to chase me.

I fumed for only a couple of seconds, and then pulled open the drawer with Ethan's love letters and e-mails on which I would base this book. It was the only stuff of Ethan's I still kept in my office because I could no longer suffer the pain of the magazine queries and book proposals he would probably never write. So I'd had those stacks removed. But I kept the letters handy for times like this.

I knew I might have to call Mr. Green, but I was only going to do it after I spent more time trying to figure out their love on my own. I hoped I could do it alone because I'd spoken to Green once before and didn't like him. I'd always been proud of how excellent I was in antagonistic circumstances, but Green beat me up pretty well.

"Miss Edwards, their story is largely one of regret," Green had said, and my teeth still stand on edge at the memory. "Ethan encouraged a simple and terribly fragile woman toward personal independence and a good career, for no other reason than he understood her desperate desire to know that feeling after a lifetime of others manipulating her. He so badly wanted both their lives to be perfect, never imagining that the career he encouraged would eventually become the only place other than her art where she knew her decisions were her own. She reveled in the fact that others had confidence in them."

"I can see Ethan helping her, but you mentioned regret. I don't see it."

"Up until the time she threw herself into work, Zelda's sickness always allowed others to lead her around, at least until she reached a point where she felt no option but to run, even if that running meant sacrificing something she desperately wanted."

"That makes no sense."

"To you, maybe. Makes perfect sense to me. Her whole life, at least up until Ethan came along, was filled with people who denied her the chance to trust her own decisions. So it stands to reason that to her, those untested decisions were unreliable. Zelda hated being exploited, but had never learned self-confidence. That made her vulnerable, creating the terrifying doubt that either accepted another person's plans for her or –"

"Put her feet in motion."

"Right. Usually at the last minute, like the two instances when it came time to marry Ethan."

"I knew Zelda was psychologically complex. Bi-polar is what I heard."

"There's truth in that, but she was way over-diagnosed as such, at least in Richard's opinion – one in which I place a great deal of faith, by the way."

"Richard your manager?"

"Who worked for years in psychology. He believes that the doctors, and Ethan for that matter, failed to understand her accompanying borderline personality disorder that made her feel so fearful, almost as though she were unworthy of getting what she wanted. Ironically, it was that tremendous fear that enabled her to make such hard and terribly destructive decisions."

"I don't know why he stayed with her."

"You could just as easily ask why she stayed with him."

"That's easy. He loved her."

"Did he ever. Even when it was hard. I remember once when I'd gone over to his house to visit. He called her at work and asked if she wanted to join us later."

"Ethan," Zelda said, so loud and firm that I had no trouble hearing from across his kitchen, "why are you calling me here? Why are you making it harder for me? You can't possibly care about my career."

"Wow, that's harsh. How did Ethan take it?"

"I wanted to walk outside and leave him alone, but as I passed, he grabbed my arm and kept me from leaving. I think he needed me for support. That should answer your question."

"For God's sake," Zelda went on, and I swear it sounded like she couldn't stop herself, that she hated the things she was saying and didn't believe them, but had no idea how to stop. "Can't you just leave me alone and let me breathe? No wonder your children hate you! You're such a control freak, hell, it would drive anybody away."

"Ethan looked embarrassed, but through it I could see him struggling for answers, looking for the right words to redirect her emotions, to help her pull out of the spiral."

"I can hear you breathing on the phone, Ethan. Now what's wrong? Why don't you say something? Is it because you know I'm right, that you don't really love me? Don't think I don't know you love your control over me, and I refuse to play along anymore. I'm going to find a man who doesn't judge me, who accepts and cares for me as I really am. Stay away from me and my girls. We all hate you!"

"She slammed down the phone. I stood beside Ethan as he listened to the dial tone for a few seconds, and then he hung up. He picked a card off the counter and handed it to me, saying 'This came in today's mail from the Zelda who is easy to love. That Zelda,' he said, nodding toward the phone, 'is a little tougher.'"

"I read the card, which had a picture of a kitten on the outside. Inside, Zelda had written that she felt so secure knowing that she had him to protect her, and that he always seemed to know, almost by magic, how to fulfill her needs, and that with him she could accomplish anything. He made her happier than anyone ever before, she said, and closed by saying she would love him forever."

"Whew," I said. "Sounds much too hard of a relationship for me."

"Hard for sure. But in some ways he was exactly what she needed, just as she was his mirror, clearly reflecting his secrets. In a way, it really was a perfect match. She was a tragically conflicted person, and you can really see it in Ethan's favorite sculpture of hers where Zelda is both the strong, defiant adult standing ready to sacrifice *and* the timid, quivering child hiding behind her and needing protection."

"I saw that bronze at Ethan's. She's both people? Never thought of that."

"Most don't. Richard picked up on it. It's a cliché to say, but Zelda was truly a tortured artist. Her work has value because it does such an excellent job of revealing her suffering."

"Do you collect it?"

"I have two pieces. My favorite is a life-sized one where she's sitting very prettily on a chair, hands in her lap and a lovely smile on her face. But when viewed from the back it's a detailed study in chaos: medications, lurking shadows, a pleading child, distorted faces and strings attached to every limb. Near the base and hard to find is a tiny replica of the front side, almost, but from more of a side view. Somehow it manages to convey a message that Zelda is always filtering the dynamics of her life, the emotional war being waged within her, so that nothing but love shows to the world at large – Ethan being the singular exception to that. Zelda often referred to the line *how he suffered for his sanity*, and that piece I love shows she truly did suffer – but less from the sickness she bore so courageously than from the people who tried to exploit it. Her work is honest about that."

"Now I feel bad for her."

"Maybe so, but even through her suffering she was generally adorable. I honestly don't know how she did it. And Ethan loved her so much that everyone who saw it stood in awe, putting her in an elite group of people who were adored – and I mean as in the purest sense of devotion. Feel bad for her if you like, but most people who knew them were envious."

"I'm glad Ethan was good for her."

"Had to be tough, knowing he could have been like everyone else and exploited her in order to have her, yet always refusing to do it. That made him the only person who really could have rescued her, and he never stopped trying, even though he knew what he was up against. He got her the job in which she took so much pride and sanctuary, and that gave her an acceptable option to marrying him – a comfortable place to run, especially since her relationship with Mike, the man who did ultimately talk her into marriage, was based entirely on her career persona, offering him little if any knowledge of the real Zelda. So as I said, both Ethan and Zelda made mistakes they couldn't find ways of undoing. Have you ever done that?"

"I don't see how that matters, Mr. Green. I'm writing about Ethan and Zelda, not me."

"That's so narrow-minded it chills me. I can't paint something I don't understand, nor would I want to. I can't put the subtle shades of bigotry into my paintings, for instance, unless I understand how subtle those shades really are. Deep emotions, Miss Edwards – passion, racism, insecurity, forgiveness, and love – don't show up as big splashes of color the way most people think. They're light touches of a double-zero brush: a look that lasts a second too long, a glance away when someone of color needs help, or a touch to the arm of a person who hurt you. If you're planning to write about Ethan and Zelda's amazing love with hammering fingers, call someone else for insight."

"Fine, Mr. Green. In answer to your question, I've made very few mistakes. I wouldn't be where I am if I did. Mine is an unforgiving business."

"In life, I mean. I couldn't care less about your job."

"In life I've made very few mistakes."

"Not in love?"

"Not anywhere."

"Then I'm afraid you're fully incapable of understanding this story."

"Mr. Green, with all due respect for your skill as an artist, has anyone ever called you an ass?"

"A few. Ethan did all the time, but he never stopped being a work in progress so I accepted it. You don't appear to be in any kind of an evolutionary state, so are you calling me an ass?"

"I just asked the question."

"In that case, I've answered it. Miss Edwards, you've never been truly and deeply loved, have you? You've never been within an emotional mile of what Zelda got day in and day out from Ethan."

I laughed, although I'm embarrassed now to admit it. "I am *very* popular."

"Wasn't the question."

"Two men wanted to propose."

"I'm sure. Loved, though, so much that nothing makes sense? So hard it hurts all the time? So passionately your life finds a new balance and you skip like a child because everything is wonderful. So faithfully that you know, absolutely, that nothing could ever make your lover think of leaving."

"I ... no."

"You want me to tell you why?"

"Sure. Take a shot." *Jerk.*

"You said you've made very few mistakes? That means you've lived far too fearfully to ever risk what's necessary to deserve that kind of love."

I would have slapped him if we'd been talking in person. Instead I slammed down the phone and took the rest of the day off.

A few days. If I couldn't get a better grip on their love by then I would reluctantly give Green another call. Maybe the screenwriter would get a handle on it first and call back with an idea.

I knew I had no business writing a love story, but I couldn't get out of my contract so by God I was going to write it. I would not fail to deliver the manuscript on time.

CHAPTER SIX - A Fool for Love?

Ethan wrote what follows soon after I took him on as a client. We were having lunch and I was trying to understand a scene he'd written, questioning his confidence in authoring the feelings of a married man. I didn't know him well enough then to understand that he kept so many secrets, so it was a surprise when he said he was recently divorced after years of marriage, and therefore felt on safe ground.

Without really thinking, and more out of bewilderment than curiosity, I'd asked what happened to his marriage. All he did at the time was shrug, but the next morning this story was in my fax machine.

Over the years I've heard Ethan say at writer's conferences that, "Inspired writers burn the passions and agonies of their life as the fuel for their stories, compelled to write until they burn all of that to ashes." I slowly learned that that was his way, particularly with painful events, trying desperately to reduce them to ashes. "It's like writing down an important phone number you've been repeating since you heard it," he said one afternoon over lunch. "Once you commit things to paper," as he had with the following story, "you can allow yourself to forget."

I'd accidentally mixed this in with a manuscript of his that hadn't yet sold, buried until recently under a pile of submissions against one wall of my office. I searched for hours to find it because I thought it necessary to include in this book. In my sleep I kept hearing Ethan and Zelda begging me to tell their story from the glorious end, but I believe it's important to know the beginning, which is why I'm starting with this vignette.

"NICE PLACE, ETHAN," my wife said as she sat across the table of an outdoor restaurant, as beautiful and in-control as she always was.

A guitarist was playing island music instead of the funeral dirges I felt more appropriate. Couples were drinking and eating and laughing, but I wasn't and my wife wasn't. Neither of us wanted to be there, and we both knew it would have been easier to keep going the way we were, getting along and doing okay.

I was the one asking for the divorce, a solution to problems I'd finally declared unsolvable because I was no longer content merely to get along, and I would no longer settle for just being tolerated. I wanted to be loved, truly loved in spite of my imperfections, and I was willing to pay a high price for a chance at it. I just wished my wife didn't have to make the first payment, with my kids making the second.

Our waiter came over, and even with all the painful emotions my wife must have been feeling as I talked about leaving, she revealed nothing to him. She smiled, asked what was especially good, and then ordered. I told him what I wanted, he left, and her smile went away. But she wasn't mad, not really. Just disappointed, I suppose. Disappointed in me, and disappointed that so many things going acceptably well were going to end. Disappointed that her life would necessarily change, and that some of those changes would be hard.

I knew she would never admit it, but she was also disappointed in herself. She had to be. I felt the same way because it was a *we* thing that was ending, not a *me* or *her* thing.

And *we* had tried hard, even though we would have had a better chance if we'd worked together. For years I'd been determined to make our marriage great, but she hardly noticed, or if she did, accepted it as the norm. It was only after she saw me give up and drift out of her reach that she too made an enormous effort that probably would have cemented me to her a few months earlier, back before my mind closed itself off to that idea. If we'd made our efforts together, would we still have died on that hill? Maybe yes, maybe no, but the odds of our survival would have sure been better.

Somebody should have told us that when we married. *Work hard together to build what you both want, because as soon as one of you settles in or quits, that's your relationship to live with or leave.*

64

"Ethan, this isn't the way I saw my life working out," she said quietly, as if politely explaining this difficulty to an attorney or judge, a thought that gave me a little stagger as the guitar player sang about the great life in the islands. I would be paying for my decision a long time. Was I sure? Really sure?

Of course I wasn't. How could I have been? I liked my wife a lot. No, I loved her. I'd forced myself to stop saying that because it clouded my thinking, but yes, sure I loved her. She was great in every way except for how she felt about me. She didn't dislike me and I never gave her reasons to distrust or be mean to me, but what was missing was that she had never learned to love me. That was far more significant to me than I could ever explain here. Maybe I needed more love than others did. Maybe I was weak and pathetic. Whatever the case, love was something I knew I wanted to both give *and* receive generously.

"No, nothing close to the life I expected," she said in near-disbelief, and I could see she wanted to cry, or scream, or maybe reach across the table and strangle me. I knew she would never do that, though, and her ability to keep things in and stay calm made me both sad and certain. Sad that the pain I was causing would be something else she would learn to hide well. Certain because that same skill was what kept her from showing me the love I needed, the love I think everyone wants.

"I know," I said. "Not the way I saw things working out either."

"I'm really mad at you for this." Then the reins slipped just enough for her to lean across the table and say, "I've been a damn good wife to you!"

Just as quickly she looked surprised, as if wondering how she got so far over the table. She sat back and adjusted the napkin in her lap.

"I know. You have."

"Is it another woman? Are you leaving me for someone else?"

"No," I lied, although it really wasn't a lie. I *was* leaving her for another woman, but the other woman didn't even know it, and I doubted she ever would. She was a friend of ours who enjoyed the parts of me that my wife found difficult, and in doing so proved it was possible to love me for me. My asking for a divorce wasn't part of some grand scheme to run off with her though. I just wanted a chance to find someone like her who felt the way she did.

"Not another woman," I said. "I just want a chance to be loved."

"You don't think I love you?"

The salads came. I couldn't eat. Why did I order?

"I think you ... we ... have confused partnership with love. We're excellent partners. We admire each other and worked well together to build our home and finances and raise our kids. But that's not love."

"You're sure."

"Yes," I said, trying to hide my doubts. What if a good partnership was all there was to love? What if I was throwing away the best possible relationship I'd ever have in my life? My wife was amazing: smart and beautiful and an excellent mother. I knew I would always think that way, and always miss a great many things about her.

I was glad I'd taken the time to think all that out in the months that preceded that dinner because I suddenly wanted to panic, to take it all back, to hide in the safety of something *okay* and forget the dream of something *excellent*. She stared at me but said nothing, and while I was second-guessing myself her eyes seemed to move on somehow, and I could see she had just that easily let me go, accepting the news I'd just delivered and in those very few minutes crossing beyond any point of return.

I hope I'm not the kind of person who put things on scales, but the hurt I caused by asking for a divorce didn't seem that much greater than the hurt she'd inflicted by accepting it so readily.

Even so, I wanted her to understand what it was I wanted. I would have hated her to think she'd done something wrong because she hadn't. Not really. She never changed from the person I dated and married, the mother of our children. *I* was the one who took a scary look inward and clearly saw what I needed. Like a blemish on a beautiful face as it looked in the mirror, her lack of love for me was the only part of our relationship I noticed anymore.

"Remember when we were dating and I modeled on that television show?"

"God, that was years ago, Ethan."

"I know."

She took a deep breath, but not to be rude. It was the kind of breath someone might take when attempting something difficult.

67

"Yes, I remember. We were very young, both working for the same company, and you took the day off to model. You've always enjoyed acting. I know all that, so what?"

"I should have paid more attention back then, but I was too naïve to realize how significant an event it was."

"You walked down a runway in front of an audience and some cameras. Big deal."

"That's not what I mean."

"Okay, then tell me, how significant was it? Looking back."

"Remember that several people brought televisions into the cafeteria so they wouldn't miss it? Everyone watched. There was only one person in our office who didn't stop working. Out of a hundred people there, you were the only one who stayed at your desk and worked through the show."

"I was covered up with assignments."

It felt weird with all the pain going back and forth, but I couldn't help but smile. She wasn't surprised, and she even smiled back.

"Even then there was something about me you resented," I said. "Don't you see? I'm leaving you to find someone who celebrates that side of me, who doesn't belittle it, because that's as much a part of me as the things you do like."

"I've only complained about your need to constantly seek new experiences. Why is it so important for you to be adventurous? Why can't you be happy with a normal life?"

"I'll never know, one of those kinds of things that make all of us unique, I guess. I'll tell you what; we'll try to switch roles. I'll be the one who stays home and skips any chance to participate, and you be the adventurer."

"That's ridiculous. You know that's not who I am," she said, and then lowered her head. "I get your point. Hard to change."

The waiter brought the food, but neither of us was hungry. A tear dripped onto her shrimp. I reached over with my napkin, and when I did she touched my hand. I was stunned to think she might kiss it, but she just held it near her face as she looked up at me.

"You know, I see so much of you that I adore in our daughters. I don't know why those same traits are difficult for me to love in you."

My god, was there a chance she understood that's all I really wanted? Was it possible she could learn to appreciate me, maybe meet me on some middle ground?

"I'll miss you, Ethan. Parts of you are awkward for me, and I guess I've made that pretty clear." She looked sad or disappointed. "I guess what I haven't said enough is that you've been good for my life. The way you always think the best of me, that's special. You're like that with most people, but maybe they don't say it either. I want you to know how much I love that quality."

Although I had no idea what to say, I was about to say something hopeful when the waiter asked if we'd enjoyed our meals. She smiled at him and he took the dishes away, leaving the bill which she picked up to check for accuracy.

The dinner was over. I knew her well enough to understand that our marriage was too.

*****

The next time I saw Ethan I suggested he expand this into an article for me to sell to a magazine. His honesty had opened my eyes to a pain of divorce I'd never considered, that a man might suffer in the process, even if the divorce was his idea.

Ethan didn't want to do it. "If I'd handled the situation well," he said, as he crumbled these papers I'd just given back to him, "perhaps I could hold myself up as an example. But I'd hurt her deeply, so I certainly hadn't done that. To be honest, I'm not sure it's possible to handle something like that well."

A few days later the crumpled papers arrived in the mail with the following note penciled at the bottom.

Molly,

I gave your idea a second thought, but I just can't see myself doing it. I'd made so many mistakes I would spend most of the article explaining or apologizing for them.

For one thing, although my wife couldn't have known it, I sat at the table wondering if her last admission might give us a chance. She did love things about me she saw in our kids, and that could have been a starting place if we'd had the courage to pursue it. We should have gone for coffee and talked, started exploring each other and opening our hearts and souls to discovery, learning each other's real needs and true desires and with luck, finding love.

If I were to write the article you propose, that's what I would suggest people did, and I'll always regret that we didn't. But like the fool I was I felt it best if she didn't know how I felt. I'd taken a bold and terrifying step and hurt someone I loved. There seemed no option but to follow it through. Otherwise I'd been reckless with her. If we tried to work it out after I'd done that, my actions that night would surely have caused its own set of new problems between us. That's the way those things work. Insidious, aren't they?

By the way, a month after that dinner I moved out of our house. My last Sunday there I stood in my closet and cried for an hour. No one knew. The house was quiet. I think my wife and my kids were somewhere else, maybe in their own closets, crying.

I isolated myself in an apartment to write and was alone for more than a year. That may explain how I could do the worst thing I've ever done in my life – steal another man's wife.

– Ethan

CHAPTER 7 - The Artist

Two precious weeks of my allotted time passed with little progress on LZ. I'd found dozens of things to keep me busy and away from my computer, even taking refuge in an aerobics class in which I had little interest at the Downtown Y.

My deadline, and my lack of understanding about Ethan and Zelda's love, eventually left me no choice but to contact Green. Not only was time running out, but Rudy, the editor who'd bought the book, called two days after my meeting with Patricia and not only confirmed her position but also augmented it with the threat of a lawsuit if I missed my deadline. Getting a book on the shelves before Valentine's Day was their mission, and I was completely out of screw-around time.

"Jonathan Green Studios, this is Richard Weedman."

"This is Molly Edwards, Mr. Weedman. How are you today?"

"Fan-*tastic*," he said, and he really did sound fantastic in a way that made me envious of people who felt that way so easily. Then he laughed. "You're Ethan's literary agent and ghostwriter, the woman who hung up on Jonathan."

I'd heard that it's hard not to like Richard, and was starting to understand why. "Afraid so."

"That was a mistake, although he probably deserved it."

"He did. I think he did."

"Jonathan's very sensitive to being exploited."

"I wasn't trying to exploit him."

"You were prying for information about Zelda and Ethan, things he didn't want to give you until you were ready. If that's not exploitation, what is?"

"I … well, whatever. Is he available, or is he in the studio painting?"

"Neither. He's traveling with the ballet that's performing his art."

"I've read about that."

We were both silent while I tried to figure out what to ask next.

"I still need to talk to him about Ethan and Zelda. I've got to get some answers so I can write the book."

"No problem. He really would love to help, but he's funny about having such personal discussions on the phone. He likes to *see* that you're communicating, and the phone makes that impossible. So you'll need to meet him in person."

"I'll go wherever he is."

"He'll be back in a week, Miss Edwards, so why don't you come down and stay with us a few days? We'll pay for your flight and put you in one of the guesthouses. You can stay as long as you need, wandering the grounds and visiting with us over meals."

"That's nice, but unnecessary. Besides, I'm sure Mr. Green wouldn't want me down there."

"Do you think I'd invite you on my own? Uh-uh. He said you'd call eventually. He asked that you come. Said that he needs you here."

It sounded like Green felt the need to apologize in person for telling me I didn't deserve to be loved, so maybe he wasn't such an ass after all. I played along and probed.

"Needs me? That doesn't make sense."

"So what? We live on forty of the prettiest acres in the nicest part of Florida. Don't deny yourself the chance to enjoy something you won't want to leave."

"I've got all kinds of scheduling conflicts."

"It's up to you. I'm supposed to talk you into coming, but if I can't, I tried."

"Very generous. Sure I can't just call him somewhere?"

"Afraid not, so I'm going to book you a trip anyway. Jet Blue has an eight-thirty flight next Friday morning. Pick up your e-ticket at the kiosk. Come, don't come, at least you'll have the option."

He chuckled, and then I was the one hung up on. I guess that sort of evened the score on the Edwards/Green feud.

Although I would still make one last (and fruitless) attempt to write on my own, I was far too desperate not to go back to Naples. The advance I received for the story – which became legendary after *Publisher's Weekly* wrote a feature article about it and the book – had unfortunately done nothing to inspire ideas on how to write it. I was certain that including Ethan's six-month-old message from Nassau made sense, as did the story about his divorce from twenty years earlier. But from there, where?

I sat at my desk and tried to determine the real starting place, the point where *this part* of their love story really began. Was it the day they met? The way he worked through her sickness? The time he said he loved her – which was my favorite part because of its innocence, although it didn't make a good enough start because it wasn't really the beginning of their love, only the two-years-in-coming acknowledgement of it.

I hated to do it, but I held my calls and locked my door and turned out the lights, then forced myself to be honest and think about what most hurt me when I read the letters in the box. The answer was instantaneous, as if it had been waiting for me to be brave enough to seek it. The *end* of their relationship was the real start of this story. Reading about Ethan's last night in Naples was so sad and upsetting to me, especially because I would have eagerly gone down to help him if I'd known. But as out of touch as it makes me sound, I had no idea anything was wrong. He'd stopped answering his phone and sending me the jokes just starting to make their rounds on the internet, but that kind of thing happened a lot when he'd disappear for a week or two, and sometimes for several months at a time.

Had I missed some signal that he needed my help, perhaps because I'd grown so shamefully immune to signals of need? I hated to consider that, almost as much as I hated to admit that I never really understood Ethan, or how to work with him, or how to get close to him. But that was mostly by his choosing. I liked him a lot and loved having him as a client, but he was always so annoyingly secretive about so many things, compounded by the way he'd vanish and then pop back to the surface with nothing to say about where he'd gone or what had happened.

But he wasn't secretive in what he wrote that last night alone in Naples. I almost wished he had been, for my benefit, not his. He sat in that empty house all day, carefully reading the precious, painful letters and poems he would put in the box and mail to me. He made dozens of notes on them, and those words told me he was suffering terribly.

It struck me as just a little ironic that I actually called his home that very day and heard the "…that number has been disconnected" message. He'd never disconnected his phone before when he left, so that was my first real clue that things were different. I should have jumped on a plane right then, and will never forgive myself for not doing so.

CHAPTER 8 - Hollywood Calling (again)

When I was a little girl my parents raised me to be afraid, as if they never wanted me to find out the world wasn't so scary, and definitely never wanted me to feel safe without their protection. I don't think they ever wanted me to trust in my own decisions and were shocked when I connived my way out of their home at such a young age. Their surprise has always been a source of interest to me, since it was their smothering behavior that so diligently sowed the seeds of my rebellion.

I never quite realized how different a childhood could be until I saw Ethan with his daughters. He loved them so adventurously that I rather wanted to be one of them. Every time I heard about the exciting things they did – kayaking for miles downriver, camping on deserted islands, practicing survival skills and shooting high-powered weapons – I couldn't help but be envious over how lucky they were.

Ethan had an incredible capacity for risk, even where his girls were concerned. "If you want to

77

try something dangerous and all you're risking is a broken arm," he told them several times as they grew up, "go ahead. If you might break your neck let's spend some time in training."

I happened to be thinking about Ethan *The Parent* because my secretary was taking a few days off to spend with her folks, something I no longer did. That was my fault, not my parents'. They were good people. They raised me, so of course I loved them. I wouldn't leave *my* boss in a jam in order to go visit them, but I suppose that was Heather's right.

The phones wouldn't stop ringing and the rest of my staff would try to keep up after Heather left. The buzz about the book had everyone on both coasts interested, but in what? A bunch of letters and notes that seemed to defy any order that made sense? To be honest, I was questioning if there was really a book there, although the publisher not only had no doubt, they'd already instructed their sales force to tout *Loving Zelda* as the lead title in the upcoming catalogue.

I was even tempted to hire a writer to help me, but couldn't answer the question of whom. *LZ* wasn't anything like a romance writer's story, not by a long shot, but it certainly wasn't a mainstream love story either. And besides, what kind of a ghostwriter hires a ghostwriter?

Someone knocked at my door, and then knocked again. I walked over and opened it.

"I specifically told you not to bother me, Heather."

"I'm sorry. I just wanted to say I'm leaving now, and that your *friend* from Los Angeles is on line five."

She started to close the door to escape my glare. I don't think I was really glaring at her, but I did need to say something about the big wet kiss her nasty boyfriend gave her when they came back from lunch.

"Heather, try to remember that this is the office of a professional literary agent. It's not a frat house and it's not the back seat of a car. If you and that man act like that again in here, you're fired."

She looked surprised, but I felt sure she understood what she did wrong. She closed the door and I picked up the phone, trying to sound confident. "Good afternoon, Frank."

"*Como estas*, Molly, how's it hanging?"

"Don't talk to me like that. It's insulting."

"Jeez, lighten up. We're working together so I'm just trying to break the ice."

"We're not working together. You're writing a screenplay and I'm writing a book."

"Well, we're both going to look stupid if they're entirely different. Listen, I think I have a handle on this thing. Ready? Ethan was the kind of guy who went big time all the time, right? So what kind of woman does a guy like that date but a crazy one? I mean, that's the story, right? A man who lives a crazy life needs a crazy woman, just for the adventure. There was nothing boring about her, that's for sure. Zelda was one roller coaster ride of a woman, and sexy as hell, too. You see those photos?"

"She wasn't crazy."

"Bi-polar, manic-depressive, whatever you call it, she was nuts."

"I swear to God if you say that one more time I'm going to fly out there and slap you."

I couldn't believe I'd said that. Was I defending Zelda in order to defend Ethan? He chose her above all the other women he could have had and would never love anyone else, so I was positive it was her love, and not her nuttiness, that brought out such devotion.

"Whoa, Molly, cut me some slack. We're just brainstorming here."

"No, you're saying stupid things and I'm getting angry. That's a long way from brainstorming."

"I asked for your help before but my phone hasn't jangled with any Oscar-winning ideas. You leave me on my own, babe, I'm going to write it the way I see it."

"You, Frank, are a prick."

"Heard that, but listen, we're both under the gun and I'm not about to go to a meeting with a treatment about a bunch of damn letters. Besides, crazy sells. Remember *Girl Interrupted* a few years back? *Big* hit. I shoulda wrote that."

"You're deranged if you think that's the story. Zelda had a tiny emotional weakness that rarely caused a problem, and the rest of the time made her compassionate. It inspired her to help others far more often than it caused difficulties, so I'd say it was a hell of a lot smaller than whatever drives you to be such an ass. We all have stuff screwing with our heads, but she was brave enough to acknowledge hers and work around it. What's your excuse?"

"Small pecker, I guess."

He laughed, and then we were both silent.

"Okay, Faulkner," he said quietly. "So what kinds of ideas have you come up with?"

"Well . . ." I couldn't believe what I was going to say. "I'm going to Naples to meet with Green. I think he can give me some direction about the complexity and devotion of their relationship. Hang tight on the love angle until then, okay, but in the meantime maybe you could explore the whole deal with her ex-husband, write a scene where Ethan admits to Zelda's husband that he's been trying to steal her away and feels bad about it. How does that sound?"

"Interesting idea. He never told him that, though. He said he'd been ... hang on."

I quickly found Ethan's letter on my desk while Frank shuffled papers, knocked something over and muttered "shit," then came back and said, "Sorry. Let's see, he said he'd tried to be honorable."

"But he was ashamed. He said so in his letter to Paul and in his note to me that last day in America. Listen to what he wrote:"

Smudge, who has seldom been out of the house, is on the sill of a window trying to convince a squirrel of her hunting prowess. The squirrel acts unconcerned as he bounds around the lawn, close to the house but never far from the safety of a tree. Both Smudge and the squirrel are pretending to be something they're not, pretty much the way I did in my letter to Paul when I said . . ."yet I have always tried to keep my feelings in check, my words and actions honorable and in balance with the friendship I had with both of you."

"Yeah, he scribbled, 'I was such a liar' underneath."

"That's right. Then you could show how futile the whole thing was by cutting to him in his empty house, knowing he should get to the party his friends had for him. It's pretty visual stuff."

The sun is just above the hammock of cabbage palms on the western border of my land. It's beautiful here and I'm going to miss it. I wish I didn't have to leave. Heck, while I'm wishing, I'll wish Zelda were coming with me the way we'd planned.

I need to get dressed soon for a going-away party my friends are throwing, a few of whom have threatened to scuttle my boat while I'm there. They think Zelda's engagement to Mike has shattered me so badly I have to leave, but it isn't the truth. The truth is I no longer trust myself.

"Then maybe show a fantasy scene of him parked down the road from her house, maybe following her as she drives away. Put a voice-over of him talking, but Frank please don't make him sound like some crazy stalker. He was a man still in love with a woman he'd lost to someone else, nothing more and nothing less."

I know all the places Zelda eats lunch, what roads she takes home, and where she buys her groceries. I could intercept her anywhere and clear away the confusion Mike caused, his manipulation that stole her from me.

And that's precisely what scares me. Even though Zelda should be with me, stealing her from Paul made me promise God and myself never to damage another man's marriage. I took that vow seriously. Given any righteous chance at all, I'd chase her to heaven or hell without a moment's hesitation, but I won't ever contribute to the breakup of another marriage.

"And then," I said, scrambling for ideas and rifling through the pages in front of me, "you know what might be powerful? Showing a glimpse of Ethan's 'other life,' the one none of us really knew but everyone suspected. On Good Morning America he said, "I've had some dangerous adventures, sure, but my life isn't really all that exciting, and for reasons of my own I choose not to talk much about it. That leads people to speculations that often supersede anything I've ever done, trapping me between the telling of what was uncomfortable or living up or down to rumors. So the best I can do is keep my mouth shut." It drove Zelda crazy the stuff he did but never explained.

"Crazy?"

"Made her mad. Made her worry. Come on, Frank, get off the crazy thing."

"What specifically? The FBI?"

"After that, the God-only-knows agencies and governments he worked for, and the terrible fear – and damage perhaps – it caused in Zelda. I know some of the war-torn nations and third world toilets he's been to, mostly because of tiny clues I've strung together over the years. He concealed himself so cleverly."

Exposing these secrets to you, Molly, is so out of character for me. I talk a lot, and I goof with people all the time, but I'm really hiding behind my stories and jokes and animation. I'm so private and secretive that I need that defense to keep people from prying. I've gotten so good at protecting myself with words about nothing that I hardly notice when I do it anymore.

"He mentions Nicaragua in one of the letters from the box, Molly."

"He was in his early twenties. I *Googled* the date. It was just two months before that CIA cargo-kicker was shot out of the sky and onto the front page of every newspaper in the world."

"Eugene Hausenfus. I remember the guy. A screenplay of what happened to him floated around here for a while. Ethan said he was writing an article for *Newsweek* there."

"Never wrote a word of it. And his letter to Zelda was forwarded by an obscure Washington agency that got it first. Now, pull away from the jungle and make the full circle back to his home on that last night."

That's why I'm walking around my empty house and wrestling with what to put in the box for you to read.

The courage to write, Molly? I guess we'll know soon enough. Ethan

"So what do you think, Frank?"

"I probably won't do the 'other life' thing here because I was already intrigued with that and have a place for it later, a two-minute scene of light-up-the-sky stuff with bullets flying. But the rest, yeah, it might work. It's still the beginning, just seven or eight minutes into the film, so it could ground what happens next, whether we go back to their past or into his future. I'll work on this until I hear from you on the love thing. Deal?"

"Deal."

I'd almost hung up when I heard him still talking.

"What, Frank?"

"Not bad, Molly. Not too bad."

"You should have come up with it on your own."

"Yeah, okay. Well, you be cool, Molly."

"Good-bye."

CHAPTER 9 - Making Love

I'd gone home that evening and actually managed to write a few pages of *Loving Zelda*. It was a nice mental journey to a quiet place in Florida while rubber squealed, sirens screamed, and trucks moaned along the street below. The writing was crap and I knew the editor would cut all of it. If he didn't, I would have to revise it until he agreed the rewrite was better. At least it would show I was working.

I kept hoping karma, kismet, or serendipity would eventually take over, possessing my fingers and producing something beautiful, but it never happened. I'd had that feeling before and could still remember what it was like, although it had been a long time. Years ago in the bedroom of my parents' home, as I penned silly fantasies about boys on the football team and guys in rock bands, the passion that moistened my lips would wet my sense of wonder, swelling me with words I couldn't hold back, clamping my fingers around my pen as I gripped the tablet so hard my knuckles hurt. My writing came fast and rhythmic then. My stories were explicit, brief, and powerful. The endings forced my hand to set down its pen and wander over my body.

I would never be able to write like that again, though, and it was probably for the best.

I saved what I'd just written, turned off the computer, and wandered through my apartment. The maid had been there that morning and so it was clean. Not that it ever got dirty. I worked a lot and therefore spent very little time at home. No one else created a mess and I had no need for pets. The art hung straight and the flowers looked real. There were no knick-knacks to add clutter. My home could have been anyone's home, and I liked that it revealed nothing about its owner. I didn't need a collection of wine corks from happy celebrations, or frames of photos where everyone was smiling, or a refrigerator covered with children's drawings, to prove the fullness of my life.

I thought about moving Maria to twice a month instead of weekly. Could I go two weeks without clean sheets? Probably not, but I could always wash them myself. The laundromat in the basement was safe enough. I didn't have to linger down there, reading a book while killing time as if hoping to meet someone. God those people are pathetic.

I took the throw pillows off my bed and turned down the covers. It was late and the building was quiet, or maybe I just wasn't hearing the noise because my writing left me feeling as though I was still in Ethan's Florida home. It was calm, and I swear I smelled a gulf breeze, even with the windows closed. I knew I was still lost in his story and fantasizing, but I was enjoying it. I brushed my teeth slowly, looking deep into the mirror, studying the age of my face before lowering my eyes to the fresher nakedness of my breasts. I washed my neck gently, then rubbed the cloth slowly down my body. I felt it all, the warmth of the water, the scratch of the cloth, the slickness of soap, the silkiness of my pajamas as they slipped to the floor.

I heard a voice heading toward my bedroom, coming down the hallway as if whoever it belonged to was comfortable in my home and knew the way. I leaned out the door of my bathroom and pressed against the jamb as Ethan walked in with his arms full of clean sheets. Zelda was waiting to help him make the bed. My bedspread was on the floor as if they'd used the bed earlier. I could only guess at that, but they'd been up to something, I knew.

"Think fast," Ethan said, as he gently threw the bundle of laundry into the air above Zelda. She didn't move as the sheets fell down and covered her.

She remained still as he stepped up to her. Slowly, as if undressing her, he moved the edges and corners, revealing little bits of her at a time. When he moved a pillowcase from her eyes I could see her happiness at being the focus of his attention, secure in the love and passion so obvious in his eyes.

"Very funny."

"Couldn't resist," he said softly as he kissed her neck.

"It's late, honey. Come on." She gently shook herself out of the linen as if it were a robe. It dropped to the floor. I stayed quiet. I didn't want them to know I was watching, and would have been embarrassed if they'd seen me. I was as rude and perverted as a voyeur peeking through blinds for a glimpse of nudity, but at that moment, the way I felt made it irresistible and impossible to stop. Although I would never masturbate, I felt just the way I did in the final seconds before an orgasm, those stiff fingered and all-devouring heartbeats when focusing and finishing become *intensely* important.

He pressed against her from behind. His lean but muscular arms encircled her tiny body.

"Don't, Ethan. I have to get up early."

I couldn't see where his hands were, but they were low, I knew that.

"Please, don't."

He was gently kissing her from behind as his hands searched her. A siren outside got their attention and made them stop. I didn't breathe and stayed perfectly still as I waited for them to look away so I could get back my rhythm. I glanced down at my anxious hand trembling low in front of me, and when I looked back Zelda had turned so that his mouth could go to her breast.

"I have to sleep," she said, but I could see she'd lost herself to him, lost herself to herself, lost herself to the things she needed, the desires all women had and the passion he'd triggered in both of us.

She lowered herself slowly onto the bed and touched his stomach, then ran her hands up his chest, exploring him. He looked at her as he leaned down and kissed her, and then looked at the ceiling, his back toward me as she disappeared below him. He breathed deep, and then moaned something I couldn't understand, a deep moan of pleasure that reverberated through my own body so powerfully that my legs spasmed. I went stiff for a few seconds. Then I was suddenly unable to stand the weakness that forced my naked bottom to the floor.

I sat there with my fingers and legs clenched together, trying like hell to keep quiet. I almost lost interest in Ethan and Zelda, almost forgot they were there until the wet and noisy sounds of their lovemaking proved too seductive to ignore.

She stopped and said his name quietly, almost fearfully, as she leaned far enough back for me to see her face. "Would this be a good time to confess something?"

"Right now," he said, "You could confess anything. I feel too good for anything to upset me."

"I was hoping you'd say that because I've got a teensy-weensy confession to make."

And then she went quiet. He waited. Both their breaths became shallow and unfulfilled, begging for more or less but not that.

"Okay, Z, let me have it. What did you do?"

I couldn't fathom her timing. Tell him afterward, maybe, or never. But not during sex. Her eyes were so full of worry that I wondered if maybe she couldn't relax with the guilt. Maybe she couldn't give herself the option of waiting. She turned her head away.

"I'm scared to tell you."

He was aching from the sudden stop of pleasure. She needed to help him. Somebody needed to help him finish. "Just say it, Z."

"Promise you won't get mad?"

His back was a fascinating landscape of small ridges and deep cut valleys.

"I'm getting mad now, so tell me already."

"I slept with Robert."

"Bullshit."

She looked down, past him, through him. "I'm sorry but I did. I feel bad about it now, but after work we went out for a drink, to talk business."

She stopped but he was waiting, naked in front of her. I could see the effect of her words on his body and I hurt for him. Who wouldn't?

"I didn't mean to drink that much, but ... well, you know I'm so tiny it doesn't take much alcohol. I shouldn't drink. You shouldn't let me go out."

I didn't want to believe her. I wouldn't believe her. She wouldn't do that to Ethan. I knew she was confused at times and occasionally mean, but I never figured her to be unfaithful.

He stayed calm, or at least he tried to. I knew him well enough to know he was furious, but would never show it to her now.

"Where did you do it?"

"This is really bad."

"*Where?*"

"In his car. God, it was like I was seventeen again."

"You did it in his car?"

"No one saw us, I swear, and I know he won't tell anyone."

He bit his lip and thought about what she said, what to do, what he should say, what this all meant to their relationship.

"Really?"

"You're mad. You said you wouldn't be mad."

"Is … it … the … truth?"

She suddenly gave up the game and threw a sheet in his face. Then she laughed and grabbed his waist as her feet drummed the floor in celebration. She was so delighted with herself that it really was cute and adorable, even though Ethan looked like he wanted to kill her and I know that I did.

"How many times now?"

He stripped the sheet of his face and muttered. "I only fall for it because I love you so much."

"No, I'm good. I should have been an actress."

"Yes, you should have been an actress. Now where were we before you had your fun?"

She was still a pixie as her hands reached in front of her and she leaned forward. "Right about here."

A minute later he was taking deep breaths, with even deeper exhales. Then she stopped again and said, "Love me, Ethan. Make love to me."

"I do. I will."

Then he left the room. I heard him open the back door to his home. I looked out the bathroom window and saw Ethan naked among the trees. Then he was back, padding softly down the pine flooring of his home.

He came into my room with a sprig of blossoms he'd clipped from an orange tree. He took Zelda's hand and squeezed the orange blossoms into her fingers. I could smell it from where I stood quietly and it was lovely, almost like honeysuckle. Then he moved those fragrant fingers to her nose. She breathed in the scent and she smiled as he used other blossoms to caress her bare stomach and chest.

He touched and rubbed her – absolutely adored her – for half an hour before making love to her. It was incredible, the most beautiful thing I'd ever seen.

After they finished I turned out the light, slipped into my bed and pulled up the covers. I could feel them beside me, the heat from their bodies and the wetness of their passion. My hands wanted to wander again but I wouldn't let them as I fought my way to sleep.

At seven, Zelda's voice woke me.

"Morning, Ethan," she said, so cute and happy and childlike.

I rolled over gently, trying not to attract any attention as Ethan hugged her and said, "I'll never get tired of waking up to find you in my bed. I never thought it would happen."

"That's a lie, silly. You always knew it would happen."

She was right. I knew he always did. He never doubted they'd be together, not once.

"It's beautiful looking at the woods out your windows. The haze as the sunlight passes through the trees. I love it here. I look forward so much to each and every sunrise."

He looked out the window at the streaked light filtering in through the pine, palm, and cypress trees.

"Ethan," she said seriously. "You do love me, don't you? I didn't leave Paul for nothing?"

"You left Paul to find love?"

"Yes."

"Do you feel loved?"

"Right now? Absolutely."

93

"And yesterday, and last year, and the year before?"

"Absolutely."

"I love you more now than I did yesterday. I'll love you more tomorrow. I'm addicted to you, Z, and always will be."

She didn't say anything, just slid back under the covers and cuddled quietly against him. In her silence I could only guess how happy she was.

I dressed as silently as I could and left them alone as I headed for work feeling good about what I'd done. If they never had managed to get together on their own, I was proud to be the one to make it happen. If only in my fantasy.

When I sat down at my desk I smiled, thinking there wasn't any chance at all that Zelda got to work on time.

CHAPTER 10 - Naples, Florida

Jet Blue flew direct from New York to Fort Myers. The flight Richard booked for me was the same one I took when I flew down to research the idea of writing Ethan's book, months before I pitched the synopsis and outline, and a lifetime, it seems, before I'd cornered myself into writing his novel.

Although it was cool in New York, I'd checked the weather in Florida before I left and packed for sunny and eighty. Richard had promised that Jonathan would pick me up at the airport for the thirty-minute ride to his home in Naples.

We were late taking off from JFK because of an injured man. It didn't look very serious to me but both his legs were set in casts, so wheeling him aboard and into a seat was quite a time-consuming ordeal.

Watching the flight attendants helping the guy reminded me of a letter about Ethan being shipped home injured. I had no idea from where, or the extent of his injuries, but I did know he was surprised to see Zelda when he woke up in the hospital in Naples.

I'd read their letters so many times by then that they felt like my own memories, almost as though the entire span of their relationship, at least what I knew of it, happened to me. I felt their thrill of being together, and the excitement of their future. Felt it so much I'd even considered how nice it would be to have something like that for myself.

Through all that reading I'd gotten several glimpses of Zelda's enormous range of emotions, from a high of incredible exhilaration to a low of near-suicidal despair. If my life was a flat line – and I've tried very hard for many years to keep it that way – hers was a bouncing ball dropped from a ten-story building. Way down and way up, making theirs an out-of-control relationship over which Ethan could only hope to have some influence,

Ethan did seem able to track her emotions, though, and could usually guess what she needed and when. He foolishly but truly believed that if he just tried hard enough he could make her happy no matter what. He learned the warning signs of her behavior and eventually became so determined to help her that he did something I would have never expected: He stopped traveling for adventures so he would always be there for her. Maybe that's because he felt guilty for causing some of the emotional crashes he needed to untangle.

They finally pushed back the plane as the man with his legs in casts looked embarrassed for the delay. I wondered if it was some tragic catastrophe that hurt him or some little mistake gone badly wrong, the kind that deviled Ethan and Zelda. Only one of their letters mentioned something terrible. The rest of their problems were minor disappointments that would never seem significant enough to cause depression if not for the euphoric backdrop of Zelda's manic happiness.

"Hey," Zelda had said softly on Ethan's second day in the hospital. She was holding his hand and straightening his hair.

He smiled weakly and fell back to sleep.

When he woke again it was dark, but there was still enough light to see her sleeping in a chair next to his bed. He watched her. She felt it. She woke.

"What are you doing here, Z?"

"Aren't you happy to see me?"

"Of course. But who knows?"

"Everyone."

"Paul? Your kids? They know you're here?"

"Everyone knows. You've always been there for me, Ethan, so nothing could have kept me from being here for you. I know that sounds funny coming from me, but I wasn't going to let myself be weak where you're concerned."

He thought about their two years of secrecy as she moved slowly toward a divorce that still hadn't happened, but was now close. He thought about the shock everyone must have felt when they came to visit him and saw Zelda standing guard. Thought about what kinds of problems it might create with her kids' perception of him.

"Scared, Little Biscuit?"

She suddenly abandoned her bravery, threw her hands over her eyes and rushed her answer. "Oh my God I'm terrified."

"I'm so proud of you."

"Really?" She lowered her hands, smiled, and scrunched her shoulders.

He reached for her hand and then kissed it. "My little rescuer. Thanks." Then he fell back to sleep.

The doctors eventually released him into her care. She checked on him every morning, evening, and lunch break. She made sure he had everything he needed, most of all her love. At one point he heard her say to someone on the phone "I do care how it looks, but not anything compared to the way I love and care about him."

One day at lunch she strutted around his bedroom as though she were making decorating decisions, so excited and happy it thrilled him just to watch her. "Guess what, Ethan. I'm going to move in."

"I can't wait for that day."

"Not just while you're healing or during the weeks we don't have our girls. All the time. My kids will move in too. Of course, you're going to have to buy another bed. I could never feel totally at home in that one."

"I know. I understand."

"I'm okay about it, though. Long time ago."

"Go out this weekend and pick a new bed. I want you here. It won't be long."

"I'm ready to leave Paul and move in now. I'm working, Ethan. You said I needed to work, and I am."

"I thought you wanted to know what it's like to be independent."

"It's not important anymore."

"It was important."

"I don't want to do it. It's too hard."

"Zelda, you've always wondered what it's like not to rely on a man. You've told me your reliance is what gets you manipulated so often."

"But I know you won't do that."

"You're right, I won't – well, maybe I'm doing it right now, I'm not sure – but I want you to know that you're bright and wonderful and able to take care of yourself. In a way, I need you to have the confidence of being self-sufficient."

"Why is that so important?"

"So you can tell me to shove it anytime you want. If you can do that, I'll know you're only with me because you want to be. That's cool. Do you have any idea how special you are?"

"All I want is to be with you, Ethan. If I have you, I know I'm special."

"Just a couple of months on your own. Just long enough to pay some bills and get confident that you can do it. I'm not going anywhere, and the experience will be great for you. It's your one chance because once we're really together I'm never letting you go."

I know Ethan was hiding the part of his heart that needed to be sure she came to him freely, choosing him from everyone on earth and not just as an alternative to Paul. Her living alone – her independence, even for a few months – was a key to that. I understood it, I really did, but God did that selfishness take a catastrophic toll, setting a stage on which they never would share a home.

Ethan watched as Zelda's excitement changed to despair. She sat down on the edge of his bed and tried not to cry or look like she was pouting. She should have let it out, but she didn't.

"Forget it," she said, her emotions swinging heavily. "You're right, I do want to be independent. I would never move in now. I was just testing to see what you'd say, and you sure didn't disappoint me. You always hold out what I want like a carrot, but as soon as I get brave enough to reach for it you snatch it away. You couldn't possibly love me and do that. There's no way."

"We want the same thing, Z. We've got a lifetime together ahead of us, and all I want is to start off right, giving a little time for the dust of your divorce to settle while you learn how capable you are."

"Ethan, if you really wanted me to live here, I'd be here. You obviously don't want that. It's just a game with you, isn't it? A hurtful game. I won't let you hurt me, Ethan. I won't."

"That's not the truth and you know it."

"I've got to go. I'll be late getting back to work."

"Don't leave mad. Let's talk about it tonight."

Although she normally would have been unable to stop bashing him, this time she managed. She truly was getting better, and maybe Ethan had something to do with that. She stood there and stared down at him, then around the room she'd just been decorating in her mind. "I … I can't do this," she said.

100

She was as empty now as she had been full earlier. I'm angry that Ethan didn't struggle out of bed to hug her.

"I have to go. Bye."

Her eyes were on the floor as she walked out of his bedroom. She was so sad it made him ashamed.

He called her at work an hour later but she wasn't there. Thirty minutes after that she was still missing. He worried about a traffic accident as she drove back to work with her mind lost in thought over his stupid plan for her.

He was desperate to find her but unable to get out of bed, so he called several friends and sent them to her home, the pier, the city dock, their favorite restaurant, anywhere she might have gone. They searched all afternoon and late into the evening but didn't find her. Around ten o'clock they went to Ethan's home in hopes of figuring out where else to look. The door was unlocked and they walked back to his bedroom.

"Why is her car in the driveway, Ethan?"

"What?"

"Her car. It's in front of the garage."

"Oh my God." He put his head in his hands as they ran out of the room.

They found Zelda a hundred feet into the woods, sitting on the ground beside the little sprig of the Hope Tree the two of them were nurturing back to life. Fire ants and mosquitoes had bitten her throughout the day, but she didn't seem to notice or care.

They helped her to the house, poured her some water, and started making something for her to eat. She silently watched his friends in the kitchen for a few minutes before wandering back to Ethan's bedroom and climbing into bed. She still didn't speak as she cuddled into him and went to sleep, a tiny, precious, wonderful woman with demons I would always blame him for setting loose in her mind. He'd totally missed the point of what she really needed. I was amazed he was unable to see something that was so obvious to me.

He held her as best he could all night, crying over his confusion about what to do, but sure he needed to do something. He loved that troubled woman more than I ever thought I'd understand, and hated being the one who so often seemed to trigger her depression, chasing away the Serotonin that normally bridged the gap between the senders and receptors of her brain. By doing that he would steal the beautiful lights from her eyes that had so much control over him. He wanted her strong and healthy, the way she was most of the time, but he loved her always. I knew he always would.

*****

As long as I'd known Ethan, I always held him in pretty high regard. I never overlooked his flaws, of which there were many, but I always thought he was a decent guy trying to be a good person. He had confidence in his judgment and the plans for their future, a future he felt sure would keep Zelda happy. He was willing to risk a lot to get them there, but he unfortunately never seemed willing to risk the plans themselves.

Although that seemed to indicate a massive ego on his part, when I took on this project my initial perception was that most of their problem was Zelda, that her sickness created so many impossibilities that no one could have overcome them, and that if anyone could, it would be someone like Ethan.

About the thirtieth time I read Ethan's notes on that letter I just described, my impatience with her began to fade, and I started catching glimpses of what an amazingly simple creature Zelda was, and why Ethan loved her so much. I also started to see why so many of his plans for her happiness failed, and that he might have been the perfect mate for her if only he hadn't been so sure he was the perfect mate for her.

In truth, Zelda and Ethan both just wanted the basics of life and nothing more: to be in love, to be together, and to combine their families. Money, career, possessions – none of that mattered much to him, and they mattered even less to her. As I sat on the plane staring at the seatback and tray table in front of me, for the first time I saw the question in her eyes in Ethan's bedroom almost eighteen years earlier: *Why isn't it enough for me to love you? If you love me back, I don't want more than that out of life. I just want to be with you.*

By encouraging her toward the independence she'd always said she craved, did Ethan want more for her than she really did want for herself? How much of it was for her, and how much for him? Was he trying to manipulate her, help her, or do both, perhaps? I would never be sure. All I did know was that he took a beautiful, simple, and loving person – a rare and treasured find – and *forced* her to change.

I wonder if I've ever done that to someone, or if someone has ever done that to me. May God forgive anyone who has.

As with so many good-meaning people, I was sure that Ethan had only the best of intentions, so it's strange how much damage he did. He introduced her to work and independence with the hope they would make her feel confident, but he surely never guessed their impact. Ethan wrote somewhere that they became addictive drugs to her, but it was only after reflecting on their letters that I saw how terrified she was by the step she'd taken, like someone who went weak-kneed partway across a footbridge. She would never get to the other side where she could be comfortable in that career, but neither could she risk the long fall if she slipped while turning around to go back to where she was safe. So the moment she started working was the same moment their chances of being together started diminishing. Seven years later her job, where she wobbled uncertainly between two reasonable options, would be the reason Ethan lost her.

The pilot announced our final approach to Fort Myers. I was in a window seat, and as the plane banked toward Southwest Regional Airport I could see the Gulf of Mexico below. The water was clear and beautiful. A boat of some kind streaked along the surface and its white wake fanned out like the train of a wedding dress. As the airplane slipped out of the sky and slid toward the ground I could see palm trees, hundreds of them, thousands probably. Colorful flowers splashed against a backdrop of green as if Florida was a place of growing and blooming and little else. No tall buildings or factory smokestacks anywhere. What a change from New York.

As the escalator took me down to street level I looked around for Jonathan and found him easily. It helped that he was the only black man I saw, but even if he weren't I would have recognized him from the pictures I'd seen online. His hair was pulled back into a ponytail, just like in the photos.

He was talking uncomfortably – listening, rather – to people he didn't seem to know. Maybe they were collectors or fans of his work. I walked over and interrupted; they excused themselves and left.

"It's a pleasure to meet you in person," I said as I extended my hand. "Thanks for the gracious invitation."

He looked surprised. It was as though he recognized my face, although I was certain we'd never met. Then the confusion lifted and he said, "What invitation? Richard told me that you insisted on coming to meet me."

I snatched back my hand. My God, did Richard set me up for this embarrassment?

"Absolutely not! He *asked* me –"

Jonathan laughed. "Miss Edwards – Molly – I'm just teasing. Yes, I invited you, so relax."

"Can you possibly think that's funny?"

"Sure. Don't you?" Although Green was almost as well known for being a recluse as he was an artist, I found him boyishly unthreatening and unfortunately likeable. Even so, I still felt a need to remain guarded. Was it necessary? I wasn't sure.

"I suppose it's a little funny. I'm not used to being teased."

"Then I'll try to be careful with you."

"I'm not suggesting that's necessary."

"It is. Probably won't be for long, though."

"Meaning?"

He ignored my question, picked up my suitcase, and we walked outside. It was gloriously and seductively warm, an unbelievable change from the grey overcast of the city. I felt like I was on vacation, and wondered when the last time was I took one, not counting writer's conferences where I earned my way by meeting struggling writers all hours of the day.

"Richard said you needed me to come. Mind telling me why?"

We got into his car. I wanted the windows down but he turned on the air-conditioning. I guess he took this weather for granted, although that seemed impossible to me.

"It's simple," he said as we rolled down the interstate. "I want to make sure you tell Ethan and Zelda's story well. They're great friends of mine. I love them, and so it's natural that I want to protect them."

"That's nice of you. I'm doing my best."

"Did you know they were going to get married at my house?"

"I got an invitation, and I certainly wouldn't have missed it."

"That's right. Been a long time ago now, so I kind of forget the details. It was going to be a major event. Just under a thousand people responded."

I was fascinated to be with Green in public because I knew he didn't enjoy it. Other than going to Ethan's house for coffee or drinks, he rarely left his estate, so of course I wanted to dig at that. Who wouldn't? "You entertain mostly at home, don't you?"

"I'd lightly painted the lower portion of her wedding dress," he said, ignoring my question, "to match a painting I'd given them, something that meant a lot to them. Zelda loved her dress. She was so cute."

"What a nice idea. The painting of the bamboo in his yard?"

"If you looked closely at the dress you could see that Zelda was surrounded by a halftone stand of bamboo, representing –"

"Their love. That's nice; she'd be surrounded by their love. I get it."

"Very good. So how do you intend to write their story? Has to be hard to do."

"It's been tough sledding so far, but dozens of their letters are so compelling I thought I might just augment them with Ethan's notes and then string them together. Kind of like a peek inside someone's diary, a glimpse at their secrets."

He looked at me blankly. His car drifted toward the other lane.

"Watch the road."

He corrected, and then looked at me again. I didn't think it was *that* stupid of an idea.

"That's it, Molly? Just the letters? Give the readers the facts like you're Joe Friday?"

"It's viable. I mean they're … have you even read them?"

"I don't have to. I know Ethan wrote beautifully to her. Sometimes when she was over at my house working in the studio, she'd take a break and tell me about things he wrote. If Ethan was around he'd always blush. She and I would laugh about that."

"They are beautiful. I love reading them."

"I don't doubt that, but their story is far too moving for those letters alone to express. And complicated. My god, they overcame so many obstacles. Everyone else, and I mean *everyone* else, would have quit. But not them. They never quit"

"Their story is rare, for sure."

"But the hope is universal, a dream we all have as though it's something we're born craving. So don't you think that's what the book should be about? I'm not a writer, but it seems to me that's the only reason people read about someone else's love. They put themselves into the story and draw hope from it. That gives them what they need to keep trying, to keep dreaming, to risk taking another chance on love. The people who loved Ethan and Zelda saw only that hope. Even those of us who caught glimpses of their terribly self-destructive behaviors admired them for their hope."

"I never thought of it that way."

"Their letters alone would only make people confused, or more likely, envious. It would be like flaunting wealth you're not willing to share. Taken by themselves, they might even cause resentment toward Ethan and Zelda." Something struck him funny and he laughed suddenly. "What a great couple of characters. Did you ever see them together?"

"Only once. Ethan was in the dumps because they'd broken up. He couldn't write, but we had a deadline on a book. I came down to kick him in the butt, but by the time I got here they were back together and life was as if nothing had ever happened."

"You sure wasted that plane fare."

"I know that now. Didn't then."

"That could have been any day of their nine years together. Everything about them was intense, more happiness than even I could comprehend, but more valleys than I could ever endure. Man, they were a long-suffering couple, but you never doubted their love. Not for one single instant."

"They sure were happy the few days I stayed. Zelda was even more delightful than Ethan described her to me. I was glad I got to know her."

"Was she sick when you were here?"

"Not that I saw, but I was only here three days. I do remember one evening when Ethan's phone rang and he bolted without explanation, leaving me alone on his porch for hours. When he returned I could see that whatever called him away had taken a lot out of him. He was as different as possible from the fun person making me laugh before the call."

"That was most likely a Z-crisis."

"He sat back down on the porch and filled my wine glass, then asked if I was comfortable. Very concerned that I was okay. Does it sound crazy to say that aside from being a little emptier than earlier, the intensity of his caring showed that whatever happened had actually added something to him?"

"Not to me it doesn't. I saw how he was with her, which was really weird if you understand Ethan. He was always kind of wild guy, capable of being so emotionally hard he could flip a switch and turn you off, a guy who wasted no time on his wounds or anyone else's. It was his strongest suit. It was also what he most hated about himself."

"That was always my impression too, that he was incredibly tough inside. But when he returned that night he was hurting and worried, and although I didn't know at the time it was for Zelda, reading their letters made me understand. The look on his face, the one I'd never seen before and couldn't come close to identifying, well, it was nothing short of devotion."

A slow-moving driver was holding up Jonathan. He passed the old boy but waved as he did. "Ethan would do anything for her. Nothing was off the list. In my entire life I've never said that about any other man in love. Ethan lived without rules or boundaries and he didn't accept them where she was concerned. Whatever it took, he gave, and he gave it happily. I think he needed to do it, that it provided something good he wanted for his life. I think … and this sounds a little out there … I think Zelda might have been a mirror to Ethan."

"How so?"

"I think she was a reflection of him, the *real* him, not the image he'd trained himself to show the world. I've had some great conversations with him, and I think he had exactly the same doubts and insecurities she had, maybe to a greater degree even. He just hid them bravely and invisibly behind a mask of confidence. I think he wanted to free her in order to free himself."

"That is a good story."

"Love, devotion, and courage. What could be better?"

"I think the letters prove it pretty well, but you could be right. To be a good book I probably need to give the reader hope, the chance to at least dream of true love."

He turned down a rural lane. At the end there was a gate and a sign that read *Jonathan Green Studios, Richard Weedman, Manager.* Inside the gate was an oasis, so incredible I couldn't believe my eyes. Acres of ornamental plants and trees, lakes, statues, metal artwork, and fountains.

"That's exactly what I got from them," he said. "Hope. Your story could give those of us who have hope a nice experience, but your real challenge, what I'd really want to do if I were you, is to give hope to those without it. I know Ethan would like that too."

"Your place is fantastic."

"It's the reason I asked you down."

"What?"

He parked and stared as if studying me for a portrait.

"What do you mean?"

He cracked open his door but didn't get out. Instead he said, "Hope, Molly. I know from our few phone calls that you're one of the folks who don't have it. I can hear the loneliness in your voice, in the words you choose to use. I hear the bitter acceptance of that loneliness in the tone you seem to find necessary. Discover hope for yourself, Molly, and I feel sure you'll discover the story you need to write. How old are you?"

I answered without thinking. I guess I was still a little shocked by his bluntness. "Forty-three."

"Then it's time to be honest. I'll help you by going first. Let's walk a little."

I forced a laugh as I climbed out of the car. "No one else is holding up their hand for the front of the line, Jonathan, so it might as well be you."

I walked beside him thinking I would never do this soul-searching kind of bullshit in New York, but at the moment it almost sounded fun. I followed him along a path, and the landscaping made me anxious to see Ethan's old place because I knew he had many of the same plants. Citrus trees splattered with oranges and limes. Banana plants with bunches that must have weighed a hundred pounds. Pineapples sitting like crowns atop sprouts of stiff leaves.

"There's another reason I wanted you to come down, Molly, something I need from you. I'll be honest about that if you'll be honest with yourself."

"Sure, yeah. Deal." I figured I could always back out later. Gutsy of him to go first.

"I need you to frighten me."

I turned quickly and leaped at him. "Boo! Like that?" Then I asked myself where in the hell that came from.

He laughed. "Funny. We could start there, I guess."

"Sorry. Trying to tease you back. Get even with you for the 'I didn't invite you' thing."

"Molly, you know anything at all about art? Where it comes from, why we do it?"

"I like to think I do. People paint or write or create poetry to express something they want to share or examine."

"That's about right, and what they create comes from inside. The best art comes from deep inside, from the very center of who we are, regardless of whether it's wonderful or terrifying or a combination that's wonderfully terrifying. With me, what has always driven me to paint is a set of deeply rooted fears. Fear of being engulfed, and subsequently exploited. Fear of poverty and hatred. Fear of seeing only ugliness, and missing so much beauty. You can look anywhere and see both."

"Interesting."

"Not interesting, tragic. Because I'm not afraid anymore. Fear comes from oppression, or at least from the risk of oppression, of being victimized. My success has removed almost everything that could oppress me."

"You're black. I would think that alone would present a lifetime worth of challenges."

"I find it funny that you're not racist. I would think you would be, but it's one of your few redeeming qualities."

"Thanks. Not really much of a compliment."

"Wasn't meant as much of one."

"Suppose not."

"You're right, though, racism used to scare me, but even that changed with September eleventh. I flew to New York not long after the attack and it was the first time I felt I was actually welcome in America. White people on the airplanes would see me sitting down beside them and be glad I was black and not Arab looking."

"God, your place is beautiful. I can't believe it."

"Let's go in and talk to Richard. That's enough about me for now, but do you see what I'm talking about? We all need things from each other, that's how this crazy old world works. Right now, I need you to scare me with your narrow-mindedness and whatever hatred fuels it. And it is hatred, Molly, that's pretty obvious, although you're the only one who might know who or what you really hate deep down."

"Zelda, on the other hand, needs you to understand her, to realize how beautifully she hid so much suffering from the world. Ethan needs you to see that he had no choice but to lead, that he had no idea how to follow or allow for any personal weakness. Together they need you to do a good job telling their story, and you need me to help figure out how to do it. The readers need you to give them hope and show them the dream, and your career needs the readers to buy this book."

"It's the circle of life," I sang badly, the catch phrase from *The Lion King*. What was going on with me? Was it him, his place, or was I going nuts? Was it because I was a thousand miles from my past? Could I have just been under so much stress in New York that I didn't realize how much I needed a break? I didn't know.

"Come on, Simba. Let's have something to eat and some wine."

I followed along easily. "Okay."

114

CHAPTER 11 - Dancing

A small alligator floated motionless in the lake behind Jonathan's studio, while an ugly duck with red blisters of skin on its face paddled nearby. Colorful Tilapia idled through the shallow waters near the bank, their dorsal fins slicing lazily across the surface. An uprising of huge boulders, covered with exotic plants, spilled water from a massive capstone ten feet in the air, the splashing orchestrated by a series of smaller rocks so that it sounded musical. Everything about Jonathan's estate was so artistic it was easy to understand why both Ethan and Zelda went there to create. Heck, it even made me creative enough to write.

The late morning sun was on the other side of the building, putting me in the shade while brightly lighting my view. I was writing this story in a large airy room next to Jonathan's studio. This entire wing of their home looked out on the lake and the alligator and the fountain through floor-to-ceiling and wall-to-wall glass. Zelda had used this same room to sculpt, and while I wrote

– mostly about Zelda because her work kept her on my mind – I really could feel her there.

Jonathan and Richard gave Zelda an unfathomable gift by allowing her the freedom to work there, to use the safety and tranquility of the studio to recreate the world that privately menaced her. Invitations to their wonderful retreat were extremely rare, even more so if they included a key and the freedom to be there unannounced, and so I had to marvel at what, beyond their art and friendship, was their reason for being so gracious. There was a connection between them I wanted to understand, but even as I worked in the same room where Zelda sculpted, I recognized it would probably stay a mystery, at least to me.

The previous night, when Richard first took me to that room, he'd suggested where I should set up my laptop, and then he sat in a chair with his Manhattan in one hand and his other hand under his chin, watching me get out my computer and plug it in. I guess his steady stare should have made me uncomfortable, but for some reason it didn't. He was waiting for me to do something, or discover something, or see something, and although I couldn't tell for sure what it was, I already figured him to be more of an observer of behavior than an influencer of it, so I felt a trust that whatever was supposed to happen would happen naturally. I'd never felt like that before in my life, and still marvel at the feeling.

I booted my laptop, and as it warmed up I looked around, for the first time really. The room, like every other room there, had lots of different art on display, but one piece immediately stole all of my attention and forced my hand suddenly over my heart – a far too feminine gesture I doubt I've ever done before in my life.

"Oh my God, I recognize this as Zelda's work."

I took a step toward it, confused and attracted by its power over me. I approached it carefully as Richard said, "It's Ethan's. We're holding it for him until he comes back. How would you interpret it?"

He joined me as the bronze continued to overwhelm my emotions with fear and hope and conflict, at the same time drawing me into its details and complexities.

"It's her best piece as far as I'm concerned. Jonathan leans toward the piece in the gallery, and then another one we own. But I love this one. Although she did a lot of smaller works after, this was her last major piece before she went to work for that stupid business and lost herself in it. She was looking for strength there, I think. Or power. Who knows?"

We studied it together in silence. After five minutes or more, Richard took a step away and said, "Zelda spent years volunteering to teach art in local middle schools. Conventional thinking is that she hoped to guide young artists away from the pain that will always be associated with her art, a chance to help others the way she couldn't possibly help herself. Most collectors know that, and therefore assume this child is someone she helped along the way. The woman, of course, is obviously her."

I kneeled down to examine the details of the little girl, holding on desperately in exactly the same way that Zelda clung to Ethan in photos of them together. But instead of the happiness I remembered from the photos, there was so much fear in this child's eyes that I wanted to stand beside the naked and vulnerable Zelda, hold out my arm the way she had and stand in defiant solidarity against whatever threatened them.

"Jonathan figured out who the girl is," Richard said. "Look at Zelda's arm, the one reaching back to comfort the child."

"It's incredibly detailed."

"Now look at the child's same arm."

I studied the tiny arm of the little girl, probably five or six years old. It was hard because her haunting stare had so much power and so much control that I kept glancing into those eyes.

"See?"

What was I supposed to see? It was all so beautiful and sad, but I saw nothing to identify the little girl. "No."

"The elbows. They both have a very tiny blemish, a small patch of dry skin at the same spot that Zelda did. I don't know that anyone else has ever noticed that. I keep it as a house secret." He winked at me. "Now you're part of it." Then he squeezed my shoulders and left me alone with the terrified people in bronze.

I worked hard all the following morning, writing about Zelda in a way I never could have in New York, while Jonathan painted in the studio next door, playing music I enjoyed a lot. Some of it was Marley, but mostly the songs were blues, some simple, and some quite stylized. The ones I liked best were complicated mixes of *a cappella* harmonies that sounded like rhythmic lowing of laborers in a field. They were wonderful.

I'd actually written several good pages by the time Jonathan came in. The interruption was welcome because the writing had eroded badly over the last hour, the way it always did when the juices ran dry. No more words strung beautifully together, and no more sentences of musical rhythms.

"Why don't you take a break? Grab some of your stuff and come with me," he said with authority, although not as a command. He left but waited outside in the courtyard.

I gathered my papers into a pile and followed him past a smaller waterfall to the main part of the house, which had even more art pieces than the studio areas: sculptures, paintings, carvings, and glass. Most of it wasn't his work, but rather art he and Richard collected together. I wanted to linger, to look at it longer, to get whatever I could from it, but I didn't get the chance. We walked through the gallery to a front bedroom, and then through that to a small patio where Christmas cacti hung on the wall. Chairs and a table with an open umbrella sat in the middle and took up most of the space.

There was a bottle of wine and two glasses on the table.

"This was Ethan's favorite part of the house. His own estate was beautiful, but quite often he'd need a change of scenery and come down here to create, to work through elements of a story or, more likely, a character. He rode his bike most of the time, huffing and puffing his thoughts into a little micro recorder as he peddled. Sometimes I'd just find him sitting here, looking out at the lake, thinking."

"It's nice he had another place to go."

"I'm sure he came more than I know. It's hard to tell when a visitor arrives by bike. Especially a phantom like Ethan."

"Are we having some wine?"

"No. You are."

"Who is the other glass for?"

"Ethan."

I was startled and I'm sure it showed. Couldn't catch it in time.

"You're kidding."

Jonathan poured the wine. "That depends on how open you are. You're better than when you first arrived, so let's test it. I'll leave you alone. There's no one else around. You'll be alone in a place Ethan liked a lot, one of the places where he bravely explored his spirit. It's still here. I can feel it. See if you can."

He touched my shoulder and left.

I thought it was nice that Jonathan could feel Ethan's spirit, but all I felt was silly. I drank some wine to make an effort, and paced the small patio wondering how much time I needed to hang around before going back to the studio to work. I rifled through the letters of Ethan's I'd been re-reading when Jonathan escorted me out there. I wondered about the answers I needed. I touched the flowers and counted the tiles across the floor. I admired the expensive outdoor table and the unbelievable landscaping all around. Massive art objects were everywhere, including a welded head with a handsome face that was ten feet tall, maybe fifteen. I sat down. I stood up. I sat down again.

A second glass of wine gave me the courage to risk embarrassing myself. I whispered to Ethan. "I am *so* pissed off at you."

No answer, of course. I looked around the estate, but there was no one who could hear me.

I closed my eyes. Opened them. Poured more wine and drank. The sun was warm and I moved under the umbrella. It blanketed me with cool shade.

I picked up Ethan's glass and checked it for lip prints. I knew he kissed his coffee cup each morning as a way of kissing Zelda, and I knew she did the same back. But no prints on the wine glass.

As I stared at the goblet I let myself mumble "I worried about you all the time down there in the Caribbean," barely audibly because I hadn't looked around again. Why was I so concerned? This place was full of spirituality.

Had I just said that? Spirituality?

"If you wanted to get away, Ethan, you should have come to New York."

I sipped from his glass, and then looked at my own lip prints. It made me feel closer to him as a breeze blew through the screen and the shade hugged me.

"My parents worried too."

I wanted to jump up and look around, but I didn't because I was sure it was just something I remembered from a letter he wrote. All the same, it felt nice to hear his voice again.

"I'm sure your kids did too." It felt even better to talk with him.

"Yes."

I stared at the chair across from me, where I imagined Ethan's voice. No one sat in it, of course, and I reminded myself that Ethan couldn't be there, even as I sat and listened to him talk. His voice got clearer, but it could only have been in my head.

"Molly, I know you feel I've wasted these years loving a woman who was never mine. A woman who finally re-married, but not to me."

"Yes," I said, mad enough at his stupidity not to care who might hear me. "I think you were a fool."

I hadn't noticed that the sun had gone down. Ethan's wine was disappearing, and as it did he slowly started to talk. He was himself, yet speaking from his heart in a way I'd never before experienced. I sadly realized he'd never really talked with me about anything important, that despite how close I liked to believe we were, I was just another person from whom he'd always protected himself with noise and babble. If something was truly important, he wrote about it, and I did feel special for being the first to read much of that. I guess I knew it was as close to Ethan as I would ever get, so hearing him talk honestly was something I'd never dared dream to experience.

"I think, all along, I understood I would never have Zelda, but I figured the chance alone was worth the risk. I got to hold her and care for her over so many years, and that doubled and tripled my reward. To be honest, I consider myself lucky, and still hold parts of her so closely it's impossible to believe they're only memories. I'm always with her and neither of us is ever alone."

"I think I'm jealous."

I shouldn't have said that out loud.

"I understand."

"I wrote you a lot of letters, Ethan. Mailed a big stack you supposedly picked up in Eleuthera."

"I read them. Didn't quite know what to write back."

"I'm sure you were still bitter about her and Mike. I was trying to help."

"I wasn't bitter."

"Well you damn well should have been."

I knew he wasn't going to respond to that. I finished my glass and poured another.

"Ethan, you have to help me. I have to tell your story right and I'm having trouble."

"I'll help you, Molly. You know I will."

"I know you will."

I filled both glasses. The bottle refused to empty, and I was glad for that.

"Molly, you have to begin by understanding that I only lost Zelda for the time being, and it wasn't even her fault. I made a small mistake and Mike capitalized on it."

I sat up suddenly frightened. Where was I? I was confused and wanted to panic, washed over with the sick feeling that I was back in the institution, but then Ethan touched my arm and said everything was okay. I knew I could always trust him, and so I relaxed.

"The mistake I made was too small to worry about, which is why I dangerously overlooked it. 'Van,' I'd said to her boss – my friend – over lunch. 'I'm going to ask a favor. I've never asked one before, but this is important.'"

I closed my eyes and sat down with Ethan and Van in a restaurant. It was a fancy place and I was underdressed. Who picked the outfit I wore? I didn't even own a skirt that short. It looked nice on me but felt uncomfortable, or at least I felt like I should be uncomfortable.

A waiter smiled and filled my wine glass. I smiled back. He put a napkin in my lap, touching my legs as he did. He rubbed one of my legs. It felt good. Better than just good. Ethan and Van didn't notice. As long as no one saw, I wouldn't stop him. His hand went underneath my dress. He was handsome and I liked him. I sipped my wine, enjoyed the waiter's hand, and tried to listen to Ethan and Van.

"Name it, Ethan. Whatever you need, you know it's yours."

"Thanks. Don't give Zelda any more responsibility."

Van stopped eating and set down his fork. Ethan asked the waiter for more bread and he left, dang it.

"Why not? She's terrific. I'm not even considering anyone but Zelda for management."

"Because you don't see the stress she already brings home. She hides it at work, but she comes home a wreck. It's killing her, Van, and I'm serious. I can see it in her art, what little she has time to do it these days. She's overwhelmed and terrified."

"The . . ." Van looked embarrassed and used his hands to gesture as he asked, "The-you-know-what?"

Ethan looked hard at him. "Do *you* know what?"

I giggled and they both glared at me, but I couldn't help myself because it was funny. Van looked the way some men did when talking about gynecology or periods, just completely out of his element. I bet if I said Tampax he would have run out the door screaming.

"Sorry," I said, and made it sound sincere enough for them to turn away. "Another napkin, please waiter." He smiled and helped me out.

Van straightened a little. "I am aware that she occasionally takes medication. Something about her nerves."

"That's right she does. And it's controllable enough at this stage. Hell, lots of people have what she's got and function perfectly. But not with as much stress as you want to load on her. That promotion will put her over the top."

"It's a good job, Ethan, and she's already said she wants it."

"Don't you see that it's professional recognition she wants, not the job. Can't you find some other way to validate how important she is to your company, because I'm not kidding, you will kill her."

Van totally ignored me but stared at Ethan for a long time and then simply said, "Okay."

I moved to get back under the shade of the umbrella. I poured us both more wine.

"So that's what broke you up," I asked. "Her job?"

"That waiter liked you, Molly. You should have given him your number."

"I would never do that."

"I know you wouldn't. Anyway, Zelda called me the next day. She wanted to quit because she hadn't been offered the job. 'It's *my* job, Ethan. I earned it and I'm the best person for it.'"

"I know you're qualified, Sweetheart. There's no doubt you've got a great career in marketing. All the clients love you, and Van told me his business depends more on you than it does him."

"When?"

"When what?"

"When did he say that?"

"Not sure, exactly. A while ago."

"You're lying, Ethan. You always pass along compliments as soon as you hear them. You would have told me right away."

"She paused, Molly, and I could almost hear the tumblers fall into alignment."

"*You* were his secret lunch appointment yesterday, weren't you Ethan?"

"Yes, Z, I was. But listen, you've got to be honest with yourself."

"You told him not to promote me."

"Van makes his own decisions. All I did was express concern –"

"She hung up on me," Ethan said as he leaned forward. "More wine, Molly?"

"Better not. Feeling funny," I giggled. "Can we dance later?"

"Sure. Why not?"

"I haven't danced since high school. I think I was good."

"Why haven't you danced since?"

"'Cuz no one asks me. Back then all the boys did. God, I was so wild. I drove my folks crazy."

He watched and waited as I reminisced.

"No one asks me anymore," I said sadly. "You never ask me."

I'd put him on the spot, and could see he was going to change topics. I needed to sober up.

"Up until this point, Mike, the guy she eventually married, was a nuisance to me but nothing more. She'd dated him when we broke up once. He knew nothing about art, and so tried to keep her focused on her business career; I suppose just to get her away from the world we'd shared. Like me, he never stopped loving her, and so wanted to stay in touch when we got back together. At first I said I didn't mind, because I've always had trouble understanding why people make the ones they love give up friends. It shouldn't have to be that way."

I pointed an accusing finger that wandered around, like a gun that would definitely miss its target. "Bang. You know a little about never stopping to love. Never stop loving. You know what I mean."

He smiled. "You're funny. I do."

"I am funny, aren't I? Why don't you find me funny more often? Could … maybe just a little more wine."

He filled my glass. I was having a really good time. I felt like everything there was just for me, that I was special the way I once thought I was.

"As I said, it's not my style to make people end old relationships, but once I recognized he meant us harm I told Zelda that 'He's a rat in our camp, gnawing at the love that binds us together.'"

"Aw, that's c-u-t-e. Maybe a tad clichéd, but *cute*."

"Yeah. Anyway, he was her daughter's teacher, and as bad luck would have it she had a conference with him the same day she lost the promotion. She was upset and he pried enough to find out why. Then he ran with it, making a compelling case for her to leave me. He said I was manipulating her; trying to keep her from succeeding; going behind her back; sabotaging her career."

"I bet that drove her crazy." I grinned.

"You're sitting here talking to a ghost, Molly. It's dangerous to throw rocks from a glass house."

"Ooops," I said, just a little tipsy. "You're right I know."

"So she came home that night and we fought. Van called the next day and said she'd quit if she didn't get the promotion. 'What should I do, Ethan? I can't afford to lose her, but I made you a promise.'"

"Van, I want her alive more than I want her successful. Give me one more chance to talk to her before you make any decisions."

"He did, Molly, but she didn't come home. Not the next night either. I looked everywhere for her but never even dreamed to look at Mike's house, which is where she was, taking comfort in his pretended interest in her professional future, a future I did not think she would survive."

"God, that had to hurt."

Ethan ignored this, as I knew he would. "Open your eyes, Ethan. She couldn't have loved you if she left so easily."

"That's a logical way to think, but it doesn't factor in her sickness."

128

"We all get sad, but we don't go out and love our leavers. I mean leave our lovers."

He grinned. He was adorable being so tolerant.

"When something like that happened to her she'd get depressed. Not just unhappy; clinically depressed, a downward spiral into a terrible abyss where she was vulnerable to herself, her emotions, and the will of people around her. I've known of people driving her to depression just to get her to do what they want."

"Now that's wrong, no question."

"God it's such an insidious illness. Isn't it Z?"

I had no idea when Zelda arrived, but she gave both of us a pixie's shrug and an adorable smile. I wanted to hug her 'cause I loved her and wanted us to be buddies. She was so beautifully tiny and petite. Ethan poured wine into his glass for her.

"Nice to see you again, Molly."

I rolled my head like Stevie Wonder. I was so-o-o relaxed. "I love you, Zelda."

She smiled. "Wow, now that's what I call a greeting. Love you too. Remember Brittany's birthday, Ethan?"

She was really talking to me, and I really did want to hear about her depression. Maybe the screenwriter was right ... a screen-*righter*? Maybe this story *was* about being crazy.

"I spread all of Brittany's presents around the living room, but before I wrapped the first one I started feeling I hadn't done enough. Molly, the more I thought about it the more depressed I got. I started crying, and before long I felt totally worthless, a complete failure as a mother for not doing more."

"That wasn't such a bad time," Ethan said as he rubbed the back of her hand. It mesmerized me and I rubbed the back of my own hand.

"I called you," she said as she squeezed his fingers. "Remember? I was sobbing and blubbering into the phone. He was twenty minutes away in the middle of a charity fundraising dinner, but he must have ran right out because he was at my house before I had a chance to look at the clock and wonder how long he'd be. He held me, told me he loved me, told me it would be all right, and then went to work fixing things."

I looked at Ethan. He was embarrassed by her praise and the attention. Zelda leaned forward as if we were very close friends.

"Not once did he tell me I was silly to be depressed, and he never showed the first sign of impatience. It was so beautiful, Molly. He smiled and sat on the floor in front of me and sweetly picked up each gift, admiring it carefully while I sat in a heap in the middle. I so badly needed him then. I'll never forget the wonderful feeling of getting better, just a little bit at a time, as he went through the gifts."

"'This is beautiful,' he said, as he got to one of the last presents. 'I'm sure you remember Brittany saying that if she only got this for her birthday she would be thrilled."

"Yes, but I got it on sale. And it's stupid anyway."

"I think she'll love it."

"Then he picked up a blouse."

"'She'll go *nuts* for this.' And then he smiled at me, knowing somehow that kidding about my craziness, bringing it into the open so I could see it as the unwanted guest it had always been would make it seem more bearable to me. He called it 'a look under the bed to prove that the monsters were handmade by me.'"

"I bought that blouse months ago. She'll hate it now. Her tastes have changed."

"Then she can return it. I'll even take her to the mall if you're too busy. I'll suggest she use the money to get her nose pierced."

"I was wiping my eyes, but couldn't help but laugh. Molly, he actually made me laugh in the middle of my misery. No one had ever done that before. Then, before I could say anything else, he said, 'Maybe I'll get mine pierced too.'"

"'Stop it,' I said, but it was just the sad part of me trying to hold on, and it was failing. 'You get your nose pierced and I'm leaving you.' I crawled across the floor to be near him."

"A neat like sword, maybe dangling off the side of my nose."

"'It's still not enough for her birthday,' I said, but by then I was just wondering, no longer certain. The crisis was over. 'I should have gotten her more.'"

"Tell you what. I'll take the tag off my present. If you still feel the same way tomorrow, give her mine too, and I'll just put some cash in my card. That will certainly be enough, don't you agree?"

"I don't think I'll need to use your gift, but thanks. It is pretty much stuff, really. More than she's expecting."

"Well, I'll take off the tag anyway. Just in case."

"Molly, I felt like a little girl in daddy's arms."

131

"Yeah?" I said. "Afraid I can't quite relate to that."

"Sure you can. Sad, but happy to have someone make everything all right. Because that's what he did. He actually made it all right. I sat there and got a grip on myself and looked around the room and realized this monster really was of my own creation, that I'd been upset over nothing, that it was once again the weak chemicals in my brain and nothing more. His love, patience, and understanding cured me without medication. It was so beautiful."

Zelda turned to Ethan and grabbed the hand he'd been using to rub hers. "You've got to believe me, Ethan, I never feel that way on purpose, and it's impossible to see it's the chemical imbalance when it's happening. When I say horrible things to you, it's not me. You know it's not me."

"I know, Z."

She hugged him and looked sad that horrible things had ever come out of her mouth. I could see how much it hurt Ethan that she hurt. He kissed her and said, "You're telling a story to Molly, and I know she wants to hear the end. We'll hug later." He tickled her lightly and she forced a smile.

"Molly, I knew I should have felt stupid. I always did at my parent's home, and when I was married to Paul. But with Ethan I didn't feel ashamed or stupid or embarrassed for being run over by emotions. He loved me so much and accepted me so easily. I felt bad about calling him and could hardly say thanks, but when I did he said it was his pleasure to take care of me."

"That's nice, Zelda. Thanks for telling me that."

She finished her wine and said, "I'm going to take a walk. Love you, Ethan."

"Love you too, Z."

Aww.

We both watched her walk into the darkness. She couldn't possibly weigh a hundred pounds. Ethan was so proud of her and proud of their love – or at least the determination their love gave them to find peace together. I could see his adoration in the way he watched her. When she was out of sight he said, "So that's how it happened. Mike confused her enough to turn her back on her one true love."

"It just doesn't sound like you, Ethan, giving up without a fight. Maybe just a smidge more wine."

He laughed and poured. "Oh man, I've never known her as angry with me as when she didn't get the promotion. Each day her anger lasted was another day for Mike to cover ground. He asked her to marry him and pressured her until she accepted, knowing she had no strength to resist. I guess he convinced her that the few months they'd dated before, along some conversations about her daughter's schoolwork, had more meaning and significance than it really did."

"Men. Ugh. Did you know I could line dance? Or maybe we could do like those kids in River Dance. That would be fun." I flung myself upright but quickly decided that river dancing might not be in my immediate future.

"I'm sorry, but I don't have much longer here, Molly."

133

His letters were almost at an end, and whatever he didn't say out there on the patio might remain a mystery forever. I focused hard and tried to listen.

"I went to their engagement dinner at Mahi-Mahi's – uninvited, of course. As his friends sat around the table congratulating them, I walked up to Zelda. The entire restaurant was quiet as I stood there and took all of their stares. Then I kneeled down so I could look her in the eyes. I said, 'Zelda, you're marrying the wrong man.'"

"Mike started to interrupt but she cut him off. 'It was always supposed to be us, Z, and you know that.'"

"Sorry to interrupt, Ethan," I slurred, "but I have to ask what Mike was doing."

"Nothing, Molly. He could afford to sit there quietly. He knew she would turn to someone else to make this difficult decision for her, and he knew I wouldn't do it. I always let her decide for herself."

"I'm proud of you, Ethan. Had to be tough though."

"He also had the upper hand because she'd told him what I did years earlier, and he really exploited it. While she was still married I'd taken a lady friend to a political function. She ended up spending the night. Zelda found out and was devastated."

"But she was still married."

"Didn't matter. I'd made a commitment to her and I failed to keep it. I could give you lots of reasons to think it was okay and you'd be convinced, but it wasn't. I know it wasn't. Mike had been twisting that knife around in Zelda ever since he found out, making her hurt all over again for what I'd done, just to take her farther away from me."

"I hate him."

"Life's too short and beautiful for hatred. Just be disappointed with him."

"Okay, then I'm disappointed with him. Big time."

"So you can imagine how surprised Mike and I both were when Zelda showed she was willing to leave the restaurant with me. I could see it plainly as her eyes softened and her head drooped and her hand crept across the table toward mine. She could barely keep from reaching out to me. She wanted me to decide for her. Damn it, that's all I had to do. Tell her I loved her, and that I still wanted to marry her. Take her by the hand and walk her away, lead her into the future we'd always planned together. But I just couldn't do it, and that's where I failed her again."

"You *screwed* up."

"I know, but all her life Zelda had been lead around by men like Mike. In every single case she eventually came to resent the people who did it. So if I made this decision for her I would not only prove I'd resort to that tactic in desperate times, but I would also risk her resenting me later. I had won her love by giving her independence, the right and responsibility to think for herself. If I took that away I'd be no better than the others. It had to be her decision."

"God, I'm sorry for how hard that must have been for you."

"Especially as her eyes pleaded with me for help. I sent every loving signal I could, projecting our history and our devotion – much more than she could ever see when she looked into Mike's eyes. I waited, wanting so badly for her to choose me while we silently communicated back and forth in our thoughts. We didn't have to talk. I heard her clearly and I'm sure she heard me. *We were meant to be together. Through all of our past and future lives, we've always been meant to be together.*

"She didn't speak as a tiny smile found its way to her lips and she looked at me with so much happiness I still remember it clearly. That's when Mike broke the trance and said, 'With all due respect, Ethan, you had your chance. It didn't work out and never will, no matter how much you might have loved each other. But she and I can make it work and you're hurting her with your interference.'"

"He stood suddenly, his knees hitting the table so hard that ice banged against glasses like a tolling of our last moment, ended. Then he took her hand and led her to the dance floor –"

"Dance floor?"

"It was obvious she didn't want to go, but just like that she was gone. She could have broken free if she wanted, and it was important to me – to us – that she did want to. But Mike never gave her the chance, holding her close and slow dancing to a fast song.

"I got off my knees then, Molly. His friends stared at me, but they didn't seem upset that I'd interrupted their celebration or created a problem for Mike. Instead they looked stunned, as though they'd just witnessed the purest act of love they'd

136

ever seen, something I was more than willing to do a thousand times again for Zelda."

"So you left? Or did you dance?" I threw my hands in the air like Michael Flattery. Flaherty? Flatly? Not sure, but I really did think I could River Dance.

"Neither. I waited at the door until the party left. I knew Mike wasn't the fighting type, and I'd sworn a few years earlier never to hurt another human being, so there was very little risk of confrontation. Besides, there was no need for any. It was all up to Zelda."

"Have a sip of wine, Ethan. Dry your eyes and drink with me."

I stared at him while he sipped the wine and savored it, or the moment, or the memory in which he was living. Hell, I couldn't tell what he was thinking except that I knew it was powerfully sad. I raised my glass. "To Zelda."

He tipped his glass toward me and nodded. He drank.

"As Zelda and her new friends passed me at the door, I said with all the love and pride I felt for this woman, 'Mike, can you live with the knowledge that Zelda and I will always be in love? We *will* be together again, so do you realize your marriage has no option but to fail?'"

"Good for you."

"It was a mistake, Molly. You can imagine how full of emotions Zelda was in a situation like that. I should have thought about that because my words turned out to be too much. She broke free from Mike and rushed out the door and into the night. I could hear her in the parking lot, hysterical and inconsolable, sobbing in a way I'd long ago learned to recognize, the kind that wouldn't stop for hours, and only then with a lot of patience and hugs, or some medication, or occasionally, both.

"She needed me badly, so I moved to go after her but Mike's friends blocked my way. They weren't forceful, and in their eyes I saw they lacked conviction for their actions, but Mike was their friend and that was that. One of them, a big guy with a shaved head, put his hands on my arms, but held me back as gently as if he were holding a baby. Someone else rubbed my back to comfort me. I believe to this day that they wanted Zelda and me together, that like so many people through so many years, they'd seen a miracle when she and I faced each other. It must have felt sinful for them to work against it.

"Mike gave me one of those 'see what you've done' looks for making her cry, and I shouted for him to go help her.

"He didn't move, Molly, so I said it again, 'Hurry, Mike, would you please go to her! Hold her tight and tell her it will be okay. Make her breathe deep, walk her around the parking lot, tell her … 'Molly, I'll never know how tears come so suddenly'… tell her I think she's made the right decision, that you're the one she should marry. Please, Mike, run out there and make her better.'

"He walked out to get his first experience of taking care of Zelda when she was sick. I would have gladly given him a hundred pointers from years of helping her, but I'm sure he wouldn't have listened. He had a harder job ahead than he could ever imagine, and as I stood there I wanted so badly for that job to be mine."

I found myself behind Ethan with my arms around his neck, hugging him for his pain.

"Then the man with the shaved head let go of me, and only then did I realize he'd stopped holding me back and was keeping me from falling. I was weak, and leaned against the wall. As his friends filed past, several of them touched me as they went by. Many of them were crying."

"God," I said as I stopped rubbing his back so I could focus on his pain. "That is so sad."

Ethan stood. He looked away so that I couldn't see his eyes. I knew he was still crying. I could hear it in his voice when he said, "Let's walk the path around the lake. Have you seen the ornamental pineapples? Z loved them."

"We'll still dance later?"

"I promise."

"Good."

We walked outside. The sky was dark but the area around us was completely light. I could feel the shade of nightfall and the warmth of the sun. It was glorious. The path was stone but didn't hurt my bare feet. I was barely touching the ground.

"A week later Zelda and Mike were married. That left me no choice but to move away."

"We forgot the wine."

"We'll get it in a few minutes."

"Why are you still waiting, Ethan? You have to go on. Life goes on. Isn't that what everyone says?"

"Have you gone on?"

"Nope. Nopey-dopey. Not me never. Afraid I'm eternally unlovable. Even you can't find a way to love me."

He put his arm around my shoulder and gave me a hug. "Your heart should move on from wherever it's at. You're missing out."

"Nope. Not gonna."

"A shame. I have good reasons for waiting. You don't."

"I think it's time to dance. And what, Mr. Ross, are your reasons?"

He stopped for a second to think. Not about the answer, but about telling me.

"My favorite is that she'll come to her senses and leave Mike, all on her own accord. She'll still have that note I gave her before I set sail and she'll call you."

"She could call *me*. Right!"

"You'll put us in touch and we'll be together again. I have no doubt we'll pick up as though we never missed a day, or even a breath. She will never stop loving me, of that I am sure, and I will never stop loving her."

"She could call *me* ... I think I just said that."

He took my hand and led me around a bush. Why would they plant a big bush in the middle of the path?

"Or maybe she'll keep slipping away until she goes completely insane – do-lolly, as she jokingly calls it, even as the fear of that probability taints her laugh – and Mike will decide she's too much work and move on with his life. I'll go home and care for her. I knew she was nuts from the beginning, and I know today she'll end up crazy. But love not only endures that, it celebrates it into something wonderful. True love does, at least. Like an old man I saw on an airplane once, I can think of no more satisfying a conclusion to my life than caring absolutely for a woman I absolutely love."

I giggled. "She *could* call me – wow that's a beautiful thought, being happy to take care of her for life. I like that."

He smiled at me and I kissed his cheek.

"Or she might rebel against the way he manipulates her. But what I mostly want is for her to get tired of hurting, of missing me. She never wanted me to leave Florida, and since that day I know she's missed me as much as I miss her. Even down in the islands, years and miles away from her, I feel how she hurts."

"I know she hurts."

"And I hurt the same way. Did you know we send each other our love to ease each other's pain? Every morning when the sun comes up and whenever there's a storm. Her marriage to Mike is just another storm to us, a bit of darkness before the next sunrise and nothing more."

"I want to dance now, Ethan."

"That's why we came out here, to dance by the waterfall."

He took my hand and he danced with me. Not since high school. So seldom in a man's arms. How come so long?

God, I must have been drunk to say things that sounded like Chinese dishes. Two orders of *How-come-so-long* and an eggroll, please. I should never drink that much, but I did like being funny again. The music ended and I sat down on a chaise in the patio. Ethan kissed my hand, and then, like warm water down the drain, he vanished.

The door to the patio opened. In the light from the bedroom I saw the empty bottle in front of me. Jonathan wrapped me in a blanket.

"Enlightened at all, Molly?"

"I dreamed, Johnny."

"Johnny?"

"Johnny. It was a nice dream."

"Get any answers from Ethan?"

"I did. It was just a matter of relaxing, I guess. Thinking about what he's written."

"Perhaps," he said. "Perhaps."

I was too comfortable to move, so I decided to sleep out there, like camping when I was a kid.

Jonathan went back inside the house. I heard him and Richard talking to a man who sounded very much like Ethan.

I drank the last sip from his glass and closed my eyes. And in my sleep Ethan and I danced some more.

CHAPTER 12 - Going Home

"Good Morning, Molly," Richard said as he closed his briefcase and put it next to some luggage by the door.

"Aspirin," I begged. "Pretty please."

"We put a bottle over by your orange juice. Right *Johnny*?"

Har-de-har-har.

"Thanks," I said, and then managed to corral just enough strength to add, "*Richy*."

I guess they found that funny because they laughed hard enough to hurt my head, or rather to make my hurting head feel worse. It seemed like a beautiful morning, although I didn't really care because I felt like someone had driven nails into my skull and then dragged me through a hedge backwards. But I also felt something else, something good that lingered from last night, or the absence of something bad that I couldn't remember. Either way, I felt better than I had in years in some hard to understand way.

Jonathan sat down at the table with me and said. "I might be wrong about you, Miss Molly."

"That's nice. I don't feel good enough to argue."

"On the phone some time ago. I said you didn't have love because you lived too fearfully to deserve it."

"I don't remember that conversation. I was probably just pretending to pay attention."

"I really thought you were like so many people who seemed determined to sabotage love by being demanding, self-centered, insecure ... I don't know, lots of reasons I guess. Untrusting. Used. Beaten up. Things that come out of fear in one way or another. The kind of things that are easy to blame on anyone but ourselves."

"Could we talk about this some other time?"

"Sure. I want to get back to work anyway. Been up all night and can't seem to stop. A fantastic feeling."

As he rose to leave I realized he didn't care whether we talked about me or not. He was just trying to help.

"Okay, maybe a little more, Jonathan. But softly, okay? Little words. Low voices."

He didn't come back to the table, but he did stop and lean against the wall between two paintings of large black women in full dresses, their colorful fabric swollen like parachutes in the wind.

"You do live fearfully, but you're also a work in progress so that means there's hope. I'm actually surprised by your willingness to change. I'm not sure you've chosen to do it, but over this weekend I've seen that something's pushing or dragging you to being better."

"I don't see it."

He thought about that while I dumped lots of sugar in my coffee. I'd always heard that sugar helped a hangover, although I had very little experience with alcoholic hangovers. Back when I was wild, drugs were my addiction of choice.

Why do I feel the need to write something I've never admitted before? And why am I letting it survive my editing.

"Maybe I can help you recognize your progress. Care to walk back to my studio?"

"I could use the fresh air between here and there." I stood up and felt shaky. "Assuming I make it that far."

"Please don't puke on the orchids."

"I'll aim for one of the potted trees."

As we started to leave, Richard said, "Give us a minute, please."

Jonathan hesitated at the door, and then said, "Sure. Molly, come back whenever you're ready. Have a great trip, Richard."

Richard watched through the glass doors until Jonathan was out of sight.

"I just wanted to thank you before I left."

I was baffled, since I felt like the one who owed him thanks. "For what?"

"I know Jonathan admitted to you that he paints out of fear. So you must understand that inherent in what I do is an obligation to keep away the things that can hurt him, yet still allow him to be fearful."

"You protect him."

"I protect him, that's right, the way I protect everyone I love. And *you* were a danger because your personality tends to be exploitive. Zelda and Jonathan shared a fear about being exploited."

He was right about me, although I wished I could have denied it.

"Jonathan is pretty strong, and can stand up to most circumstances that frighten him. Zelda," he said painfully, like a father who'd lost his little girl, "wasn't nearly strong enough."

"You both loved her, didn't you? Just like Ethan loved her."

"Jonathan sure did. I never allow myself to get involved to that degree. Anyway, I just wanted to say thanks for inspiring Jonathan. The works he started to create last night are going to be amazing, and you're the one who scared him into it. He sketched five canvases. In twenty-five years of watching him work I've never seen him so wonderfully creative, his years of experience yoked to the inspirational fears of a beginner."

"Then I guess you're welcome."

We stood there for a few seconds, and then I suppose he decided he'd said enough. He walked to the door and picked up his bags. As I turned to leave he said my name and that made me stop. He stood with his back to me. "Yes," he said, with his bags in his hands and his posture squared solidly against the outside world.

"Yes?"

"I tried hard not to love Zelda. I knew how she suffered, and I don't like to suffer. But that's part of what love is about."

I was so moved by the power of his confession that I wanted to go over and hug him, but in truth he intimidated me a little because his wonderful manners were no match for the very tough little man I knew they concealed. So I just stammered out what suddenly seemed obvious to me about

Zelda. "She drew so much humanity out of Ethan, too. Maybe that was her role in life."

"Maybe."

I felt like mentioning how shallow my life seemed in comparison to hers, but it too felt obvious so I didn't say anything.

"I'm ashamed that I kept her out for so long," he said, and then he left. As his limo pulled away I thought about how deeply Zelda had touched both Jonathan and Richard, and how enormously she'd affected Ethan. As I walked past hundreds of plants in dozens of species I realized the value of what she gave all of them, and what Ethan and Zelda together gave so many people. I'd always thought their friends held them up as a perfect love, but they didn't have perfect love, not by any stretch of anyone's imagination. What they did have was genuine love. I guess the difference can too easily seem insignificant.

I felt myself slowing as I moved through the courtyard and toward the studio with thoughts of Zelda wandering through my mind. Flowering bromeliads hung in baskets on the wall while Jonathan waited patiently on the other side of the glass door.

"Change comes out of loss, Molly."

"What?"

"Whether it's intentional, like someone choosing to get rid of their prejudices, or as unintentional as an accidental death, loss is like fire. It creates new things in the process of destruction."

"Not quite following you."

He led me across the room and reached behind a stack of blank canvases, then pulled out a small

147

painting. "Absolutely no one else has seen this painting," he said. "I'll never put it up for sale, either."

He looked at it without showing it to me.

"I saw this woman struggling at a grave once."

"You said you were going to show me my progress. I guess that means you think I'm struggling."

"I'm sure of it."

"You're that smart?"

"You tell me. I was inspired to do this painting after I'd taken flowers to a friend's grave. The woman in the painting was already there so I waited a short distance away. I tried to look in other directions and respect her privacy but I couldn't stop staring as her grief seemed to build until it triggered something inside her. I interpreted what I witnessed as a fight for both the end and the beginning of her life. Not life in a medical sense, either, but rather a life she saw possible if she could only wash away the emotional damage of her years and start over as open and unguarded as a baby. The damage she'd incurred through life was trying to yield to faith that her life would be beautiful if she'd only trust it to be. She played out her powerful drama in front of my eyes, and made me feel so bad I came home and painted her."

"So she didn't make it?"

"She wanted her *hurts* to die at the grave of someone she loved. She didn't want to die, she just wanted a death from her past, from whatever the grave highlighted back in the years left behind her."

"It's so hard to start over."

"That's what I saw. The fear of trying for a fresh start. Kind of like you feel this morning, unless I'm way off the mark."

"I'm just hung over."

"The woman at the grave, no, she didn't make it." He stared at the painting with a lost look. "She was terrified about doing it, which meant she must have been closer than ever before, close enough to really see how scary it was to leap and then hope the net would appear. She couldn't quite do what was necessary for what she desperately wanted. I believe I captured that."

"You don't need to show me the painting. Just hearing you talk about it makes me understand."

"I want you to have the painting, Molly. I hope it helps in your own evolution, perhaps serving as a benchmark of your progress."

I didn't want the painting, even though it had to be worth a lot of money, but Jonathan stuck it in my hands and left. I was certain I knew what he'd painted so I didn't look. I told myself that I never would, that I could never stand to see all that pain caught on canvas, that I would just go back into the main house and say "Interesting subject" and move on. But it was all a lie.

When I finally got the courage I was horrified. I dropped the painting and turned away, held my stomach and took a few steps toward the door before I doubled over and vomited onto the tiled floor. I couldn't seem to stop as I vomited last night's wine and yesterday's food and something that felt like a horrible kind of blackness, a tumor of self-protection that had slowly and certainly been killing me for decades.

I left Naples a few hours later and couldn't get back to New York fast enough. It was as if the entire story of Ethan and Zelda was suddenly coursing through me and looking for a way onto paper before the pressure subsided or was overwhelmed by fear. I made notes on the plane like a professional, trying to think in scenes and sequences, of inciting incidents and turning points, of rising drama and crisis and climax and finally, resolution. My master's degree in creative writing had conferred upon me volumes of knowledge about the styles, confines, and structures of storytelling, but Ethan and Zelda's story seemed determined to tell itself in its own way. It intended to break all the rules I'd ever learned and by God I was going to let it. As long as I did a good job of delivering the theme – its beautifully simple message that we all have the chance to find love – I trusted readers to forgive the unusual telling. They might even come to love it. Who knew?

But as anxious and excited as I was to get it on paper, I couldn't go straight to my apartment or office. It was almost impossible for me to wait, but if I was really going to write their story I needed to remove my own obstacle first, a childhood that painted broad strokes on my own life – the dominant colors impossible not to see that bled into shades too subtle to notice.

As with the woman in Jonathan's painting, my past had completely distorted my view of what I really wanted in life, perverting my thinking so much that I believed love was unattainable, especially for me. Just like the gauzy shroud of past sins entombing Jonathan's wretched woman at the grave, I had to shake loose and be reborn or my past would not only hold me back, it would kill me. I desperately wanted whatever bright colors of life were still available to burst through for me, and for that to happen I had to do the most reckless thing I'd ever done. I was encouraged by knowing that Ethan would be proud of me.

I rented a car and drove to my parents' home in Connecticut. White blossoms covered the Bradford Pears and Daffodils sprouted from the ground. I saw robins in the trees and realized that they, too, were just now returning from the south. I liked the symbolism and felt emboldened by it, as though I was doing something perfectly natural.

I hadn't driven that road in more than two decades, and I was both sad and glad for that. I knew I might never drive it again, but from that day on it would be my conscious choice, a decision I made in my mind instead of a dread that festered wherever it is those awful things reside with such intimidating power. I'd always thought what happened in Connecticut was nothing more than my past, but looking at the painting made me realize that it had tainted the entirety of my life – my *life*, damn it – with fear and shame and a destructive mix of self-loathing and self-protection. Home was where I'd forged the terribly lethal edge I'd wielded so long and skillfully, but that had never protected me. Instead, I'd spent all those years using it to harm the people around me, and ultimately, to harm me. It was tempered by the same fear that seemed to motivate Jonathan, because, like me, he had a little sickness himself. In his case, though, his fear of the many shades of ugliness inspired him to find beauty, whereas I'd never been able to focus beyond the ugly.

I kept thinking about Ethan and Zelda and Jonathan and me and just about everyone else I knew as I drove home with such reluctant determination. Where I was emotionally right then, it would have been easy to believe everyone was sick to some degree, some just a little and some quite a lot. In many cases – abuse, past hurts, fear, divorce, mistakes, and betrayal – that sickness could easily defeat our need to give and receive love, and in truth it seemed amazing to me that any of us could ever open ourselves to the risks necessary to find love. Life's experiences can so easily tease us into building walls that keep away happiness much more successfully than they shield us from danger. I could only now recognize those walls as my enemy instead of the protection I'd always assumed, and I wanted nothing more than to shatter them, to crumble those solid barricades to dust and expose myself as a living, feeling human again, just like Jonathan showed in his painting.

I was finally going to overcome that enemy of my life, no matter the price. Like an alcoholic refusing to take another drink, I was dead-damned determined to beat the disease that infected my happiness. I was glad to know I wasn't the first to have that kind of struggle, that Ethan had suffered with sickness too, yet had beaten it completely. For him it was selfishness, an infection caused by so few demands on him. Everything came easily to Ethan, a guy lucky enough to be intelligent, witty, white, and popular. Beyond that, no one he loved ever needed his help, so he could afford to be selfish until Zelda's sickness cured him completely. Through her he learned how to give. Then he learned to love doing it.

Once I'd learned to understand their relationship, I could also see that Ethan had not only been infected with selfishness, he was also sick with fear, which probably was the real reason he needed Zelda so much. He overcame it in the end, but that was at least a decade too late. I'd read his professional commendations so I knew he had truly heroic moments, but as I drove home I suddenly suspected that all during his life he was motivated by fear and his determination not to give into it. Once he realized he was afraid of doing something, he gave himself no choice but to do it. So didn't that fear of not being brave in some ways make him a coward?

I believed it did, and so I guess that also made him a coward with Zelda. If he hadn't been so afraid of being hurt he wouldn't have needed proof that Zelda wanted to live in *his* home, and not just any home other than Paul's. They could have avoided all the fights and pain her career caused if he'd just had enough faith to try it. If that's not cowardly, what is?

At the same time, he was brave enough to risk Zelda's independence, and brave enough to chance losing her rather than manipulate her. His fear of making a mistake by leading – which, ironically, was probably the thing he did best in life – gave him no option but to do a courageous thing, allowing her the freedom to lead herself. That it turned out to be wrong in the end might not have been his fault, I just don't know. He was learning how to love, to give the person he loved the room to be herself. If nothing else, at least he was brave enough to try, so I won't judge him beyond that.

When it came right down to it, I guess I believed that Ethan's attempt to outmuscle his fears was exactly what I'd been trying to do. When Jonathan said, "I remember when Ethan could mentally throw the switch on someone and make them cease to exist," I sadly recognized how proud I'd been for so many years of my own ability to do that same cold-hearted thing. It was clear now that I hadn't been stronger than my fears. I'd merely been hiding from them.

I couldn't always throw the switch. I remembered holding my arms open to the entire world and being loved in return, cuddled as a little girl and cooed over and pampered by everyone. Decades had passed since anyone had pampered or loved me or taken care of me, but I still had a chance to change, to open my arms once again and take a crazy bold chance on life.

Damn I was excited about that. I had unbelievable concerns and tons of questions, but one question was particularly vexing as I drove home: Since most of us were sick in one small way or another, and sick people hurt others the way Zelda sometimes hurt Ethan, did that sickness entitle the world to love them less and avoid them as pain-causers?

Or was it possible the opposite was true? Weren't sick people – the wounded and damaged and frightened and mean – in some ways deserving of more love, not less? Everyone, at one time or another, has hurt someone who loved them, and yet they always hoped to be loved through the hurt they caused. And if that was our hope for ourselves, shouldn't we be willing to give it to others?

I turned onto my parents' street and had about one minute to accept the answer to that question. It was clear, but difficult, so I cast around for alternative answers about why we don't love others through the fears with which they suffer, even as we expect them to love us through ours. Maybe we're afraid their fears would frighten us; their hatred will blacken us; their bitterness hurt us. Maybe that's because we've all been infected with some degree of insecurity.

In one of his books, Ethan wrote a character as saying, "I have this theory that the taproot of our human experience is nourished or poisoned by our insecurities, those gnawing little wounds and fears that drive us to despair or excellence depending, it seems, upon the timber of our particular personalities – hard, gnarly, soft, flexible, or whatever."

I never liked the line and encouraged him to cut it, but now I was glad he hadn't. Perhaps we truly were propelled through life by our insecurities, the little sicknesses that make us pretend to be comfortable alone, smile with false confidence when we walk into a room of strangers, or tell someone we're anxious to see that it's fine if he doesn't come over. Those are far easier ways of handling things that scare us, and far less risky than saying hello to a stranger or telling the person we love that we're really anxious to see him.

I parked in my parent's driveway and remembered Zelda writing about finally outrunning a reputation she no longer wanted in her last letter to Ethan. That's where I was right at that second, exactly how I felt. I looked into the scary recesses of my past but could no longer see any semblance of my old reputation. Instead I saw a grown woman, a successful professional well respected in the world of publishing. It had been years since sex-starved boys honked out front or called my parents' house throughout the night. Any pictures still in existence bear little resemblance to the woman I'd become, and all the girls who hated me were probably too busy with babies and husbands to care anymore. My hair was short, my contacts tinted, and my look far too severe to belong to *that* kind of girl.

Unfortunately, I saw that another reputation had taken its place, a far more recent one I now wanted desperately to out-distance. A lifetime ago I was shunned for loving too much, but I'd gone so far in the opposite direction that I was now shunned everywhere for not loving enough, for being cruel. It was a much worse way to live, and I will no longer be that person. I have the power to refuse.

The tree I'd climbed as a little girl had grown so big I could barely believe it. I was too young to remember when Jack planted it, but I still had good memories of hiding in it and reading books under it.

I could see through the upstairs window they'd painted my bedroom. It was a different color and I was glad because the old color would have faded after all those years. Everything that happened there should have faded with time. Most of it probably had. What was still with me was there by my own choice, a burden I'd elected to carry quietly and never cure. Until I saw Jonathan's painting.

I had no idea how I'd be received, but I was sure at least my father was home because I called from the airport but hung up when he answered. The front door looked smaller. The yard was still dead from winter. The bushes were big enough to shroud the house when they filled out in the summer. Nothing looked the same, yet all of it did.

The handle turned when I was ten feet away. I stopped. The door seemed to drift open. I shifted on a crack in the concrete.

In the shadows of the foyer my mother stood half hidden by the door, as if ready to use it for protection. She looked at me as though I might have brought trouble. Her eyes went to my car and examined it, then looked closely to see if anyone was inside.

"Hello, Molly."

"Mother." I could see nothing of the loving woman I left behind in the severity of her look.

"Rather surprised to see you coming up the walk." Her voice was as flat and dead as the yard.

"I'm sure. Is Jack home?"

Her brows pinched together and she closed her eyes for several seconds. I remembered her doing that the day I left twenty-seven years ago. Some things never changed.

"Your father is in the back. He's getting the pool ready for spring."

She didn't invite me in. That was her decision and I respected it. I stood there silently, knowing that last week I would have barged right past her.

No, I wouldn't have done that. A week ago I would never have gone there.

"Did you want to talk to him?"

"Yes."

"About?"

"Both of you. I'd like to talk to both of you."

She was still protecting him. That would never change, but maybe that wasn't so bad. I was open to new ideas.

She didn't say anything else, just turned around slowly and walked away, leaving the door open. I followed her. It felt unbelievable and uncomfortable to be back there, a place I swore I'd never return.

The same mahogany table was in the dining room. I remembered it stacked with all my things three weeks after my sixteenth birthday. I could still hear me crying. I still saw the police standing close, and felt the caseworker's hand on my shoulder. I still saw my father in handcuffs, my mother close to him.

As I walked through the house I heard me shout the word *molester*, and looked around as it echoed off the dark walls and low ceiling of the hallway. My mother didn't seem to hear it, but then maybe she'd heard it echoing through her home for so many years she'd learned to ignore it, along with the hushed whispers from people at the club and the loud taunts from the kids along the street, a street she would never leave because it would be quitting. Running.

Molester. What an ugly, ugly word.

My mother walked slowly ahead of me, as if still undecided about putting me face to face with my father. I wanted her to walk faster. I wanted out of that house. I wanted to get it over with. I wanted so many things I could not come close to expressing.

"Jack," she said, and there was a warning in her voice he recognized. Through the windows I saw him look up worried, as if he'd never stopped expecting the police to return, never dropped his guard against the suddenness of trouble. He set down the skim net and waited. He saw me in the shadows of the interior but certainly couldn't recognize me. He was in the bright sunshine and I had trouble recognizing him. He was so much older, and not just in years. He was older in an abused sort of way, the way people age in prison. Although my charges were never proven and he'd ultimately been released, all those years under such ugly suspicion had piled hopelessly on top of each other until they equaled a life unfulfilled.

"Jack, Molly is here." Her voice the sound of bad news delivered.

He rubbed his wet hands on his pants and stood there. I wanted to run away, but I wouldn't. The way to love was through recklessness, which is the exact reason I came straight from my flight. A sudden, decisive action. Maybe foolish. Maybe lots of things, but I was too close to my goal to waste time worrying about that.

I stepped out into the light. He didn't move. I stopped. We stared at each other the way enemies might. Enemies in a war neither wanted to fight anymore, but one with no easy roads to detente.

His face was stone, not hard so much as fixed. His mouth didn't move. I read nothing in his posture or expression except a confirmation of the confusion in his eyes.

He was wearing shorts, probably the first time this year. His legs were white. They'd bowed a little more. I remember mother and I teasing that he looked like he rode a horse to work. I smiled slightly at that memory and it confused him even more.

Mother left me standing alone and moved to his side. She didn't take his hand or touch him, but she was ready to protect him. Anxious to protect him. I was proud of her for that.

Should I make a joke about his legs, like in the old days? Should I blurt out what I wanted to say? Should I start with my newfound belief that sick people deserve more love for their sickness, not less?

I didn't know. I walked around the pool and stopped a few feet away.

I'd forced myself through plenty of awkward introductions in the past, and what they'd taught me is that if I opened my mouth, something would come out. Usually something okay, but meeting my father again was so important I didn't want to chance something idiotic, so that risk I did not take.

All three of us stood there. A breeze blew and he shivered. My mother rubbed his back. It was time to cross the battlefield that separated us. I took three steps toward them.

No one spoke.

I opened my mouth and "I'm sorry" came out.

After that I couldn't do anything but look at the ground. Ants made a tiny trail in front of me. An old stain blemished the pool deck. His bowed legs moved his feet in my direction. A step and then another. He was close to me.

"It's good to see you," he said softly. "I've been worried for so long."

I couldn't look up. I was crying and couldn't let him see that.

"I'm so sorry, Dad."

"You should be," started my mother, and just as quickly I saw my father's hand leave his side. I know it went up in a signal for her to stop. She did.

"It's okay, Honey," he said to me, his voice full of the soothing I remembered as a child. "Long time ago."

I stood there ashamed of what I did to those people to get out of their house and away from their interference. My father's entire life was destroyed by my lies. Arrested, fired, leered at, and ridiculed over a child's vengeful allegations, my juvenile reaction to his "controlling my life," which is what I swore at him when he took me out of school to put me into rehab, and banned the friends I partied with.

My mother could have left him, could have taken half his money and moved on to a brand new beginning. But instead she allowed me to destroy her life too. She loved him that much.

Love. My God I have missed so much.

I didn't look up as I asked, "Mother, do you think you can ever forgive me?"

More silence. I saw my father's feet step back. Then I saw them come into view again. Mother's feet were beside his. We were still silent. I forced myself to look up, and in her face I could see decades of pain and shame and humiliation festering through the demands of her daily routine. Two lives destroyed. Three if I count my own. Yet there we were together again. I didn't blame her for hating me. God was she struggling.

"I don't know," she said finally, with a hard edge that sounded amazingly similar to my own, the cold and clinical way we both protected ourselves. "Molly, I just don't know."

My father took her hand. She squeezed it hard. I could almost see the life it energized in each of them.

"Sweetheart," he said to her, so quiet and gentle it broke my heart. "This is our daughter."

My mother shook her head no. "Our daughter is dead to me. Years now."

Silence. More than a minute of it before my father said, "No, Ruth. She's not dead."

I hoped he'd come over and hug me, but I knew he couldn't. He needed to stay with the woman who stood beside him through all I'd done to them. He was holding one of her hands, but used his other hand to reach toward me. Absolutely, totally, unlovable me.

I felt like his hand was a lifeline, something I desperately needed to grab in order to survive. I was terrified of taking it.

I heard Ethan say, "Risk! Take the risk. For God's sake, Molly, take —"

I snatched my dad's hand and took a step forward. He was surprised. My mother leaned back. I was close enough to hug them, but I wouldn't.

He squeezed my hand too. I saw him squeeze my mother's. I knew he wanted us to be a family again. God, how could he find the strength to do that?

Mother pulled away and walked uncertainly toward the house. She was confused over what to do. If it were up to her I'd be gone, no question, but she loved my father. She wanted him happy. I suddenly realized she was exactly the way Ethan was with Zelda, both willing to do anything and everything necessary for the ones they loved.

She stopped at the door and turned around. There were tears on her face but she didn't seem to be crying. Her head was still proud. Her posture was stuck in the defiant pose that my lie had forced her to master. She made the tiniest pretense of a smile and said, "We'll be eating soon, Molly. If you'd like to stay."

She went inside. My father was worried and wanted to go to her. He also wanted to stay with me. He wanted us all to eat together. What a simple goal for a father to have, one meal together as a family.

It was as though I was sixteen again, hurting my father for trying to help me, shaming his name and throwing away the dreams he had for a little girl no longer innocent, not by a long shot. Yet standing in his unconditional love while I did all of that to him, a love I'd only recently come to value.

"Hungry?"

"A little."

"Then you'll stay?"

The skin of his hand was rough and I wondered what kind of work he now did to make it that way.

"I just didn't know how to undo it, Daddy. It was so hard to admit I lied."

"I know, Little Bunny. Would have been hard for anyone. You'll eat with us?"

"I'm sorry it took so long."

He seemed to consider all that right there in front of me. I watched his mind wander over the years as his eyes seemed to memorize me. Then I saw him make a decision. It crossed his face and took the strain from his eyebrows. In that instant he closed that painful book. I could actually see him do it. He had decided that my coming back home was the end.

And the beginning.

CHAPTER 13 - The Last Message Ethan Ever Sent, an E-mail from Nassau, Bahamas on November 17, 2004

Dear Molly,

First of all, let me thank you for doing what must have been difficult. I have always been inattentive to your affection because of my love for Zelda, but that doesn't mean I didn't receive the messages you sent so subtly. Telling the woman who called how to contact me ran counter to your own desires and that makes it noble.

The Bahamians I'd hired to clean W*aiting* made her look and smell better than she has in years. I was thrilled to see the salt spray washed from her rigging and the oxidation polished off the fiberglass. She still bears the scars from her long years of service to me, but those scrapes and dings now look like exceptions instead of the norm. It was really a mess, much the same as I was before the barber shaved off my beard and cut my long hair. This evening I look much like the clean-cut guy I was when I last saw Zelda. I'm older, of course, and weathered from the sea, but I wanted to make sure she recognized me –

165

though I'm sure even blindness couldn't keep us from feeling it when we were in each other's presence.

I found a photo lab on the island that reproduced the picture of Zelda and me that I mounted on the bulkhead the day I bought this boat. Do you know what they can do with computers now? I was amazed and excited by the results. Salt air had badly eroded the old one, but the kid at the shop made an enhanced copy that looked as good as the original, at least as I remember it. I think you have a copy of the photo I'm talking about, where Zelda has her arm around my neck and I'm leaning into her and our faces declare to the entire world that we're crazy in love. It's a wonderful picture from a Christmas party, I think. Wish I could remember who took it so I could send a thank-you gift.

I also had the kid print you a picture of me taken this morning. If you use it anywhere give credit to Patrick Byler Clark, the guy whose boat is next to *Waiting* at the marina. He introduced himself and said I looked too happy not to photograph. "Some people shoot sunsets and animals," he said, "but I shoot pictures of joy. Can I take yours?"

I was flattered, but not surprised. When you get the photo I'm sure you'll see why. Man, was I a happy guy, just about to shower and pull on my new clothes and get ready to see Zelda again.

Molly, did you ever get around to reading the letters I shipped to you ... gosh, what's it been, nearly a decade ago? Can it be that long? Anyway, there was some mention, I believe, of a blue dress with white polka dots. My apologies for my vague recollection of what I did and didn't tell you, but the dress is so important I feel sure I wrote about it.

This morning, after the sweet Bahamian lady gave me some fruit and a flower for Zelda, I finally took the dress out of the freezer bag I'd stored it in when I packed up my house. I've saved it for this very day, just before I saw Zelda again, so I could fill my nostrils with whatever lingered of her perfume as a sort of ceremony before her arrival, a celebration of a reunion that should have never become necessary.

Then I waited for the woman I'd dedicated my life to loving.

I admit I was getting pretty discouraged as the morning slipped into afternoon, and then slid ever further toward evening. I was also hungry because I'd asked them to toss all the stale food, and didn't have anything else on board except the fruit the lady had arranged too beautifully to mess up.

As evening approached I told myself that her flight might have been canceled as a precaution against the hurricane that got closer throughout the day, the wind blowing harder by the hour. It didn't calm at sunset, which is unusual in the tropics, and *Waiting* strained at her lines as she lurched up and down in swells that made the harbor feel like open water. The wind howled through the rigging with an ominous sound, as if blowing bad news that traveled stubbornly. I tried to ignore it, although I confess I could not, and scared myself with all kinds of interpretations of what that bad news might be.

It was still light, but just barely, when a man walked down the pier toward my boat. He was a big man who walked with timidity, as if determined to get somewhere he was scared to go. Although the wind blew from behind him, a glance at his face made you think it was pushing him back.

He checked the name on my boat and then said, "You're Ross, right? Haven't changed much."

A floodlight behind him made it hard to see details, but I could see he'd aged gently from the last time I saw him, leaving Mahi-Mahi's to comfort the woman I so badly wanted to take away from him, the very woman he stole from me. It would have been fair, and for so long now I wish I had, although it would have required me to break a promise never to do that again.

I stared at him for a long time without speaking, trying to think of any reason for his presence other than the obvious and terrible one. Maybe Zelda was back at the hotel. Maybe they'd agreed to split up, and he'd come first to discuss how to best handle it so that one of us always held her safety net. Maybe he'd left her and wanted me to know so I could go back and take care of her.

But I couldn't convince myself of any of that, and since I didn't care at all about Mike I almost went to the cabin to suffer alone. But he'd come a long way to tell me this in person, so I would respect him for that. I would have a lifetime to grieve later.

"Mike," I said, my voice cracking as I waited for the worst news of my life. "Surprised to see you here."

He looked away and I saw he was crying. "This is going to hurt, Ethan."

His lip quivered. He put his hand over his mouth to hide it. Barely realizing what I was doing, I stepped onto the pier and put my arm around him. It felt strange, Molly, almost as if he and I were suddenly a team. Two men who loved the same woman more than anything else in life, and who would both suffer her loss more than I had the strength to imagine.

I led him to a bench nearby, in front of the rental boats the owner of the marina was securing with extra lines. I helped Mike sit, but didn't myself. I needed to be on my feet. Although I haven't actually seen Zelda in ten years, I've slept with her every night and woke to her every morning. I've had coffee with her on thousands of sunrises, and started each of those days by sharing a kiss with her. I've asked her how she liked the flying fish, the secret coves, and the circling porpoises. Asked her over and over when we would be together again.

I never expected this to be the answer.

I managed to stop trembling long enough to say, "It was another woman who called my agent to find me, right? Not Zelda?"

He nodded his head. "Zelda died," he blurted out, and then started sobbing. He hugged his knees and rocked himself like a baby, saying it over and over. "She's gone, she's gone, I've lost her."

I closed my eyes and turned away. Then I burst out crying in a way I never had before. It erupted in me with violence and shot through my body like all the goodness I'd worked so hard to store was escaping. Maybe my soul was ripping away from my life and chasing after Zelda, I didn't know, but it hurt, physically, as if I was being torn to pieces. The part of Zelda I'd carried for so long seemed to be fleeing my life to join her in death.

I sobbed and cried and he did the same and I didn't think we would ever stop. The marina owner walked over and tried to help. He touched me and I hugged him in a way I've never hugged another man. I needed strength, anyone's strength, but my grief must have been too terrible because he hurried away as soon as I let go.

I was weak and helpless when I looked up and found the worst part of the storm and pleaded, "God, please don't let her leave me. I'm begging you not to take her from me. I haven't touched her again the way I always knew I would. I haven't held her hand or made her laugh or pretended not to find her funny for so long, and I *need* to do those things. God, please, please don't take her yet."

There wasn't an answer, so I put the message of my heart into the wind. "Zelda, you can't leave me now. I have plans for us I've not yet told you. Dreams of yours I've yet to fulfill, and an old age of wheeling you around and taking care of you. Don't leave until I can do that for you. Don't. Please."

Suddenly the noises stopped. Wind driven waves had banged boats into docks all day, making so much racket I'd stopped paying attention, but now all that stopped. It was eerie, and for a few seconds I wondered about the eye of the hurricane. But we were just now getting the leading edge and the eye was still far away. It felt that calm, though, and in the hazy periphery of my vision I saw people stepping out of buildings, easing cautiously into the open as if they expected a trap, fully aware this couldn't possibly be happening.

But it was happening. God and Zelda were both listening to me. In my mind I could almost see her turning to God, tilting her head the cute way she always did and asking him for the favor with that cute smile on her innocent lips, fully expecting him to do it for her – "I need you to stop the wind, God. 'Kay?"

And why shouldn't He? He gave us our love for each other, and He had to share our joy in something so genuine and beautifully created. He had to be crying too for taking her away.

It was so silent that even Mike lifted his head to see what was happening.

And that's when the gentlest breeze moved across me and I heard her in the rigging. The wind had been moaning wordlessly through the shrouds all day, but as I stood there crying and begging and aching and dying I heard Zelda's sweet little voice, carried by this heavenly breeze and teasing me from the wires.

"I would never leave you, Silly. I never did, and I never will."

"I love you, Z."

I have no idea how long the calm lasted, or that Mike and I stayed there in silence, bound by

171

this woman but separated by everything else. I remember the final, deepest shade of darkness settling in but little else besides my tears.

I felt very strange, alive and dead, alone yet hopeful. I'd lost something when my body erupted, but hearing her voice made me wonder if that hadn't been necessary. Maybe I had to lose the part of me that belongs to this earth. Maybe – and I know this will sound strange – maybe the pain I felt was death. My body no longer suffered from my fall off the spreader bars. My heart no longer ached for Zelda. I felt strangely not of this world, as if I were a part of it but yet detached, a foreigner, a ghost.

Then I heard Zelda say, "I love you so much," but it didn't come from the wires this time. It was a human voice that came from Mike's direction, so I turned around confused, convinced I'd heard her from heaven but thinking she couldn't have died and still be here talking.

"Mike, did you hear that?"

"I said, she loved you so much," and I understood it was him I heard, his words and my thoughts distorting each other.

"I know," I said, looking back at *Waiting's* rigging and hoping to hear more. "She must have loved you too."

"I think she did. I like to think so. But nothing like the way she loved you."

His honesty overwhelmed me, and in it I saw my darling Zelda, who was so frankly honest it was sometimes embarrassing. Mike was reflecting the glorious effect she'd had on him, the kind of effect she had on everyone who knew her.

Mike hadn't seemed to hear Zelda when she spoke to me from the rigging, so we were sharing this tragedy from such entirely different places it made me feel bad for him, and like him just a little. "She had a lot of love," I said. "It probably just felt like more because it was mine."

He liked hearing that, and I was glad I said it. He was hurting, Molly, hurting badly. He'd come all this way to tell me his wife had never stopped loving me. I can't imagine how hard that must have been. I could afford to worry about him because although his Zelda had died, mine was more a part of me than before.

"She got up early every morning and watched the sun come up. No matter how late we stayed out she never missed it."

"That was our time, Mike. We always started our days together. Even when we were dating, if I was away I'd face east in the morning so we could watch the sun and have coffee together."

"Our house faces east. Over the water. It took me a few years to figure out why."

"She would have told you. She didn't keep secrets."

He shrugged a shoulder and used that arm to wipe his eyes. "Didn't really want to know, I guess. Made no sense."

It was all so simple to him. He loved her while she loved me. Whatever you think about the challenges Zelda presented me, Molly, you have to know that only an incredible woman could deserve so much devotion. Mike and I would have locked arms without a second's hesitation and thrown ourselves over a cliff to bring her back. How beautiful is that?

173

Neither he nor I said anything for a long time, maybe thirty minutes while I stared down into the water. I have no idea where he was looking, but eventually he touched my arm and said, "Here."

I took what he offered. It was only the size of a credit card but I recognized it instantly. She had taken the letter I'd given her when I left, the one with your number on it, and reduced then laminated it.

"She carried it with her all the time. I never asked about it."

He was struggling harder than any other man I've ever seen.

"She stayed with you all these years, Mike. She knew I wanted her, that she could come to me whenever she wanted, but she stayed."

"I know. I made it easy. You two had lots of problems. I try to avoid problems."

Even with teary cheeks and a runny nose, I couldn't help but laugh. I hugged him and said, "Mike, you have no idea how many problems we had. I'm sure we're still legends back there for the number of times we split up."

He rubbed his eyes and laughed a little too. "You are. Still legends, that is. Must have been something to see."

"Amazing we survived."

He looked surprised, as if marveling how I could ever think that we'd survived. "Yeah. Maybe I should have dealt with some of the problems better than I did. I guess I might have allowed her to die by ignoring them. That's the way I feel, anyway."

"I think she and I pretty much gave it a full effort, and the problems were still there. I doubt she had much energy left to keep trying, so no point in thinking that way."

"She was fairly docile with me."

I think back on the Zelda I lost ten years ago, wonderful, occasionally crazy, but always animated and never anywhere in the same galaxy as docile.

"Wow, never dreamed I'd hear her described that way."

"Does sound funny, knowing what everyone tells me about your time together. I'm jealous as hell over the great things I hear, but the problems? I would never have wanted them."

Then as quickly as it had stopped, the storm started again. People who'd crept out of boarded-up houses ran back inside for safety. I felt scared again, terrifyingly lonely, as if the calm and Zelda had gone away together. I wanted to fight it, and so I placed all my confidence in what she'd said, that she would never leave me.

Waiting didn't look at all inviting as she pitched against the waves while the wind whistled through her rigging without saying a word, but it felt right to make the offer to Mike. "You want to come on board? Might be more comfortable, assuming you don't get seasick. Rockin' like hell, but dryer, certainly."

He was tempted, but scared. He'd probably read the laminated card a hundred times, and certainly knew that *Waiting* was always an option to his wife, a home with another man who loved her, a ready escape that only required her to get on a plane. What a burden that must have been to a husband. He looked down at *Waiting's* sharp bow as it rose and fell on the waves, slicing the water as if eager for a chance to sever him from Zelda.

"Nice looking boat," he said flatly, still looking at the bow's clean re-entry after each wave. "Think I'll pass."

"I understand."

Then suddenly he looked up at me. It was a hard look for such a gentle man. "Ethan, the doctors said she had a heart attack. Figured you'd want to know."

"I was always worried about her heart. It beat fast all the time, like a bird."

"Want to know what I think? I'll tell you anyway. I wrestled with this all the way down and decided already to say it. She died – " he broke down and turned away, but then came right back at me. "She died because her tiny little heart didn't have the strength to keep beating so far away from yours. She half died when you left and she never got over it."

I didn't think I could stand to hear any more of that, so I walked away but he followed, hurting me with his words as if they were the only weapon he could ever use on another person. Then he grabbed my shoulder and spun me around.

"You probably weren't even out of the harbor before she knew she'd made a mistake leaving you. It was like her folks died and she'd been told she had cancer on the same day, she was that unhappy about your leaving. After a year I even offered to try and find you for her, if she was sure it would make her happy again. But hell, you know her pride, and it wouldn't allow such a thing. So she just started dying. There was nothing I could do. She lost interest in her career and quit to be an art volunteer in the schools. Then she quit that, too. She was seventy-eight pounds when she died, and I believe most of that was the weight of her broken heart."

I reached out to comfort him but he jerked away.

"You bastard! I'd rather had you around our house and her be happy. But you selfish son of a bitch, you *left* her!"

I did not want the words to stick but they did, and left me with no idea what to say. How do you answer a man who accuses you of killing someone he loves? Had I really done that? Please, God, don't ever let him convince me of that. Don't ever let me believe him.

Mike looked like he'd never raised his voice before, and for a moment I thought he might hit me. Then he took another long look at my boat and turned to leave. I was worried about what he might do. I've seen far more than my share of dying men, and I've seen acceptance in the eyes of some of them and a hope for the end to come quickly. Mike had that same look.

"Don't leave yet, Mike. Let's go somewhere dry and talk."

"I'm done, Ethan."

"What will you do? Mike?"

He glanced at my boat again and then looked at me. "Do? What, with my life? I already have, Ethan. I already have." Then he shuffled away, down the pier and into the night, moving along with a few people heading back to higher ground.

I'd lost most of the goodness I'd felt after hearing Zelda's voice, and stood there for a long time feeling bad, feeling lost, feeling alone, God, so alone. Even on the saddest nights with the darkest skies in the widest expanses of ocean, I'd never before felt so alone.

The wind blew harder and the rain started. I didn't move. The wind was so strong the bare poles of my boat were leaning twenty degrees. I had trouble standing, but still I didn't move.

And then over the howling wind I heard her again, as clearly as I've ever heard anyone, her pain for my pain carried along with her words.

"I'm here, Ethan. Please stop crying. Sweetie I love you so much."

Molly, I'm sure as you read this you'll want to worry about me, about what I might do in such an unearthly state. Please don't. The weather is worsening by the minute and only a fool or crazy person would venture out to sea with this hurricane coming, and I can promise you I lack the courage to be either.

I do have a request, though, one thing I'd very much appreciate your doing for me. Dig out those dusty letters I sent you so long ago and try to make some sense and order of them. Augment them as necessary with things we've talked about since, and then give them to her kids and mine. The good and the bad, the parts I'm proud of and the parts that still shame me, because the truth is that the love Zelda and I have is worth whatever price we had to pay for it. Maybe our kids will learn something from us, so that if they ever get the chance they won't make the mistakes we made. Who knows? At the very least they'll know their mother and father were loved completely, and how lucky is that? I wouldn't trade my life with Zelda's love in it for everything else this world could offer.

You've always been a good friend to me. Thanks for that.

Ethan

CHAPTER 14 - Where This Book Actually Began

I got home late the night of Ethan's last e-mail, which he must have sent within an hour after Mike left him crying on the dock. I tried to call the marina in Nassau but the phones were out. CNN said the Bahamas were taking a terrible beating, with winds reaching 150 miles an hour – the high end of a Class 4 hurricane. I was worried sick and up all night, even as I tried to trust Ethan to think of his family, his career, the millions of people who loved his books, and his friends numbering more than any other person's I've ever known.

He never wrote again. I managed to talk to someone at the marina the next afternoon and learned that right at the worst of the storm, Ethan cast the lines off *Waiting* and fought his way out of the harbor and into open water.

Without much thought, and before that week ended, I did as Ethan asked and put the box of his and Zelda's letters in a package to their kids. That was long before there was any talk about a book, and so I pretty much figured that would be the end of it. To be honest, I was glad to have them gone. I was so angry with Ethan that for the first time in almost twenty years I cleared my office of his manuscripts and articles and replaced him with a new client, a slightly dispassionate but workmanlike writer of innocent books for children.

All of that was a mistake. Ignoring my sadness was what cracked open the door to the very grief I wanted to avoid. I didn't know it then, but feeling that pain and emptiness was the first step in my process of opening myself to love, the catalyst that eventually forced me to explore ideas for this book and make two painful trips to Naples. It would also lead me from the airport to my parents' driveway several months later.

I'd always prided myself in my ability to compartmentalize pain, especially emotional pain, but I guess losing Ethan just hurt too much because I didn't really work for almost a month. My second week back in the office Ethan's oldest daughter called and asked if all four daughters could meet me in New York. I still wanted to be alone as much as possible but agreed to meet them, largely because I'd seen Ethan's daughters a few times before and liked them. I was also interested in meeting Zelda's girls. I knew the four of them had been friends since shortly after Ethan and Zelda met, so it sounded like an interesting diversion from my solitude and loneliness. I hadn't been out with a bunch of girls in years, and although they were much younger than I it still had that kind of feel to it.

Just before lunch the four of them came into my office in a pack. I stood, and as I did they all walked over and hugged me. Perhaps I'd been in New York too long because I was overwhelmed by their affection, although it did feel wonderful. They were so happy with me for fulfilling Ethan's request, thrilled to have a chance to read about the love they'd witnessed first hand – the occasional pain but incredible passion their parents erupted in each other. Each one of the girls agreed that the love had shaped their lives. Even in the worst of times, they said, there was never any doubt that something incredible existed in that relationship.

Two of the girls were married, and although they readily admitted they'd fallen a little short on what their respective dad and mom had found, they laughed and said their marriages were still good, and far better than their friends' were. "Just seeing what was possible raised the bar a lot," said Brittany, Zelda's youngest. "Much higher than it would have been normally, so I know I'm better off because of what I learned from them about love."

Ethan's oldest nodded her head. "I think, to be honest, we've both got Mike and Zelda kind of marriages. Still a pretty good thing. Did you know Mike never came back from the islands after seeing my dad?"

Zelda's two daughters suddenly looked both sad and proud at the same time.

"I didn't, no."

"None of us ever heard from him again. We couldn't find him, either. No idea what happened, but I kind of feel like he took my dad's place down there, waiting the way Daddy did. For Zelda. To truly learn how to love. Who knows?"

The other two, one daughter from each family, were marital holdouts. They would find the love they'd seen, they were sure. They had no doubt and no willingness to settle, and in their eyes I could see Ethan's stubborn, smiling determination that seemed to will things to work out. I believe Zelda must have had that same trait.

Those girls became family that day, which to me was an almost forgotten concept. I'd passed along a gift of letters to them, and they gave it back to me with the hope that I'd tell this story. They said that people expect so little from relationships anymore that they needed a reminder of what true love really was.

At first I wouldn't even consider it, but then I remembered Ethan's reason for sending me the box: "Perhaps among these scraps and scribbles that mean so incredibly much to me, you'll find the inspiration you need (to write your own book)." So that's where this book actually began, long before I flew down to see Jonathan and opened myself to the exhilaration and terror of my own hope for love.

I wasn't willing to invest much time in this project until it sold, so all I intended to do on my first trip to Naples was get enough background information to write a synopsis and pitch letter to send to my best publishers. It seemed like an easy approach, but it turned out to be much harder than I ever imagined as each day exposed more questions than answers, more things I needed to know and understand about Zelda, her years with Ethan, and the profound impact she had on him. I thought I knew Ethan pretty well, but I never lied to myself that he always held back from me how much he loved her. I guess he worried that he could never make me understand. As with so many things important to him, he never once tried to explain their relationship to me.

I remembered dozens of times when he couldn't write, and when I asked him about it he'd say his muse was gone, that he and Zelda had ended their relationship and he might never write again. The first few times I took it seriously, and once, as I told Jonathan on that last trip to Naples, I even flew down to get Ethan back on track. I learned much too slowly that their break-ups never lasted long. Until that last major split, I think there was only one time they ever separated for more than a week.

If Mike hadn't taken Zelda away they probably would have continued like that into old age and the grave. It was part of the dynamics of their relationship, I guess, and I doubt I'll ever understand it, or be able to explain it, so I won't even try. I did question Ethan about it once, saying that if I ever had big problems with a man I dated, the relationship would be over because I didn't have time for the hassle. He didn't argue, but just said, "Then you've never had problems with someone you adore."

So there I was, sitting in my New York office after the girls left, knowing I couldn't do a decent job on the synopsis unless I believed in their love, but living a life too busy with other projects to squander several months on a tragedy, even Ethan's. In an attempt at compromise, two weeks later I took off for a weekend in Naples and went to some of the places Ethan and Zelda used to go, and did some of things they liked to do. I talked to people who saw them together and tried to decide for myself if their love affair was some kind of fatal fantasy of Ethan's, or if they really had found that rarest of all elements.

To be honest I felt a little perverted traveling from Manhattan to poke around in the lives of two other people – one of whom I'd met only once – and their relationship that, as far as most people knew, ended ten years earlier. What was I going to find?

I took a paper restaurant menu with me. It had been in the box and had some handwriting on it I think was Zelda's. I also took the photo of them dressed up at a Christmas dinner party, sitting at a table with her arm draped around his neck and both of them so happy. It was actually hard for me to look at that picture because it's obvious that Ethan got *mystical* things from her.

Mystical? I would never have thought I'd use such a silly-sounding word, and I've tried hard to edit it off this page during rewrite. I checked my thesaurus and searched all the knowledge of my lofty education without finding something better, so there it is. Whatever bound Ethan and Zelda together came down to that. Their relationship was nothing short of mystical, and the picture of them together left no doubt.

After settling into a hotel along Tamiami Trail, the first thing I set out to do was find her grave. I wasn't sure why, but it felt like I was retracing this story from the end so it seemed to make sense.

As I said, this was months before I ever had that first, antagonistic talk with Jonathan, otherwise I would have asked him where it was. I visited every funeral home in Collier County looking for Zelda Richards, which was Mike's last name. I also checked under her maiden name, but no one had any records of that either. Because

185

of her family's prominence in New England, it made sense that they'd flown her body back there to a family plot. I decided to go there in a month or two, maybe driving up on one of the first warm weekends of spring.

Their favorite restaurant was still at the address on the menu, a comfortable locals' place on the water. I sat down and ordered dinner, and when the waitress had a minute I showed her their picture from the Christmas party. I think it's the same one Ethan framed and mounted aboard *Waiting*.

"Gosh, yes, I remember them. Wendy served them most of the time. Let me get her."

I was almost finished before the middle-aged Wendy came by.

"Mind if I sit?" She asked.

"Please."

"I hustled my diners and gave one table to Eric. You want to talk about Ethan and Zelda?"

"I'm surprised you remember. It's been a lot of years."

"Could never forget a couple like that." She smiled. "Gave us all hope. Owner would sometimes comp their meals, it was just so nice having them here."

I scribbled a note in my pad as Wendy watched.

"You another reporter? Been quite a few through here."

"I'm his agent. Working on a book. The magazine articles don't seem to tell the whole story."

"Okay, but just to be honest, I'm not claiming to know Ethan well. I'm not sure anyone did, although he made everyone think they did. What makes me kind of different is that I know a little about what he was like before he met Zelda. He used to come here alone. He was different back then."

I stopped writing and tried not to show how intrigued I was by a glimpse of *before*. "Different?"

"Yeah. I guess ... I've thought about it a lot, and I guess I mean he was normal, like me. Probably like you. A little hole in his soul, you know. Then Zelda came along and filled it completely, filled it so full he was just – overflowing." She laughed quickly, and for just a second I saw the young and attractive version of her sneak out. "I saw the contrast. Nobody else I know saw him both ways."

"Wasn't he happy before?"

"Oh I think he was happy. He would come in and kid with me. Sometimes he'd edit something he'd written. Occasionally he'd bring an Arabic newspaper and read it for hours. He taught me how to write my name." She took my pen and proudly wrote something, starting on the right and working left.

"Arabic? I had no idea."

"Weird language for a blonde, blue eyed American, huh?"

"Sure is."

I admired what I assumed was a translation of her name on my pad. "Very nice."

"He was nice like that. So friendly you had to remind yourself he wasn't a flirt, just a super nice guy. Then Zelda came along. The first time he brought her here, I tell you it was like he'd come out of a coma or something. As animated as he was before, he just glowed, radiated, I don't know how to say it. It was like there was a light behind him all the time after that. Her too. My God they were special."

As I made my notes I couldn't help thinking that this woman glowed too, as if it were contagious. Zelda and Ethan had definitely touched her in a wonderful way. As proud as I was of succeeding at such a difficult career, I found myself just a little bit jealous of Wendy the waitress.

We talked for over an hour. When I left she picked up my tab. I'd never had that happen before.

I bought a street map of Naples, found the road where Ethan lived and then the house he built. It seemed somehow historic to me. It was the home he twice altered to accommodate Zelda and her daughters. The second time, he quit and sold it before the remodeling was finished. I wanted to know about that.

I stared at the address on the mailbox, the numbers I'd written on envelopes for years. Then I looked around and saw that the place was pretty much the way I remembered from being there once before.

From the street I could see some of the trees and plants they'd talked about in letters I didn't include in this book, little love notes filled with excitement about squeezing their own orange juice and growing their own vegetables. I turned off the road and idled down the long driveway of the estate, got out and knocked on the door. No one answered. It was strange territory for a woman from the city to be interloping so far off the street, but my motives were pure so I didn't see anything wrong with walking around.

A dozen citrus trees were blooming and smelled wonderful. The stag horn fern she'd given him was massive, probably six feet in diameter and hanging from a tree by a heavy chain. The stand of giant bamboo was spectacular. It was one of the first things they'd planted together, and they were so excited about it.

It took a while to be sure of the two things I most wanted to see. One was something they called the Hope Tree, which I finally decided was the sprawling tree with giant leaves. Zelda brought it home from work when it almost died. They cut it back and nurtured it, and its survival through such a hard time always seemed to be an inspiration to them. It really was beautiful.

I stared at the ground around it, wondering where, exactly, Zelda sat for hours in the grip of depression, found long after dark by Ethan's friends. I wanted to hate her insidious sickness, but I had trouble doing it. Maybe it was just intuitive, but even back then I knew it's what motivated Ethan to become such a good person. That made hating it pretty hard to do.

The other thing I wanted to see was the Family Tree, something the six of them had chosen together at a nursery and planted in a ceremony Ethan told me about. Like the Hope Tree, it too was beautiful.

I couldn't find the garden they'd planted, although I could guess about where it was. Someone had plowed it over years ago, and only grass grew there now. I was disappointed by that.

189

The owner turned into the driveway as I walked back to my car. He stopped and got out.

"Morning, ma'am. Help you?"

I walked over and shook hands. "I'm Molly Edwards, Ethan Ross's literary agent. Did you buy this house from him, or have there been other owners?"

In the slower culture of the South I thought my question sounded pushy, or none of my business. I was about to rephrase, but he didn't need me too. He smiled.

"Yes, I did. My wife and I did. Been about ten years now, I guess."

"There was some construction going on at the time? A large area being remodeled?"

"You know a lot, ma'am. Yes, Mr. Ross told me I couldn't change the work he started for a year. Gave me a good price if I agreed."

"He never cared much about money."

"No, didn't seem to. He wouldn't sell to me right away, you know. Not 'til the end of that year."

"I didn't know that."

"No-sir-ee, he was adamant that he be able to move back if the woman returned to him."

"Zelda?"

"Sure, that's her. Pretty famous couple around here. Around everywhere, I 'spect. I'm proud to live in their home."

I loved that he still thought of it as their home.

"Mr. Ross and I agreed on the terms while we stood in the driveway. It was right about where you were when I pulled up just now. We'd been walking the grounds, and I know he liked me and my wife. He was one of those guys who let you know when he liked you. Didn't ever say it; just let you know. Anyway, he said, 'If you want to buy our house, live here for a year. No rent. Pay your own utilities, that's all. If she doesn't come back to me, we've agreed on a price already. If she does, well ... you understand.' Then we shook hands on it. All there was to it."

I wished I'd told Ethan what a financial fool he was. Right after I hugged him for it.

"It was a good deal for us." Then he looked sad. "Man never came back. Never saw him again. His attorney closed it for him."

We looked around together, and then he asked. "Is Mr. Ross okay? I'd love to see him again."

"He's fine," I said. "Never better."

"Been rumors about him in the hurricane–"

"I assure you he's fine."

"That's good. Then would you give him a message for me? Tell him thanks."

"Thanks?"

He smiled big, his face happy as if from incredibly good fortune. "My wife and I had given up on ever getting pregnant. First time we made love in this house ... well –" he looks embarrassed and proud at the same time. "That's little Z's bicycle over there."

"Little Z?"

"Wife's idea." Then he shook it off and looked ashamed. "No, that's not the truth. Both of us wanted to do it."

"It's a good name."

"Think so too."

There was a grapefruit tree beside him. He picked a nice one and handed it to me. As I took it he said, "You know, others come by here.

You're not the first, not by any measure. And not just reporters, but regular folks too. It's funny because at first Becky and I had trouble understanding why they came, but somehow we always seemed to know them right off. It's like there's something binding us, like Ethan and Zelda gave each of us a little piece of a precious gift."

"After all this time?"

"Yes, ma'am. Matter of fact, some have become pretty close friends. Yet new folks come every year. I see some girls sometimes out on the road I think must be their daughters. I'd love it if they'd stop in."

I felt like I was talking to the devoted caretaker of a precious shrine. "Thanks for your time," I said. "It was really nice talking to you."

"Piece of history, that's what this place is. Want to take some of it with you?"

"I don't know what you mean."

"Walk 'round back with me, okay?"

I went with him to a worn little plant nursery that didn't look as old as the house. Ethan never mentioned it so I assumed it was added after the year expired.

"Here," he said, and handed me a pot with some tiny sprouts sticking firmly skyward. "It's bamboo, from the stand of it they planted together. I give 'em to folks and it makes 'em happy. You'll have to keep breaking it back or it'll outgrow the pot, but for some reason it doesn't seem to mind. You can't kill it. Guess there's some symbolism there."

"I would have to agree. Thank you."

"Welcome."

I was staring at the bamboo when my cell phone rang and a gentle voice said, "Miss Edwards?"

"Yes."

"I'm the funeral director you spoke to yesterday when looking for the grave of Zelda Richards."

"Yes, I remember."

"I recognized the name Zelda immediately when you said it, but not Richards, so I assumed it was someone other than a rather famous client of ours. That's why I couldn't help you. But I dug around in the records and it turns out that Richards was her husband's last name. He buried her under her maiden name, I suppose. Not really sure."

"What name was this Zelda buried under?"

"Ross," he said. "Zelda Ross."

I choked on my own voice as I said "I'm on my way."

*****

The cemetery was so pretty I thought I might want to be buried there someday. It had the nice salt-smell of the Gulf of Mexico, but instead of the palms and pines I saw everywhere else in Naples, it was full of old growth trees like back home in New York, their falling leaves a magical anomaly in Florida.

It was raining a little, so I wore my long coat as I picked up a plot map in the office. I knew about where I was going, and as I walked in that direction I was pretty sure that Zelda's was the grave a dozen or so rows ahead. Even two months after her death, it had more flowers on it than anywhere else in the cemetery. Lots of different arrangements and lots of different kinds. I knew Zelda loved flowers. Apparently everyone knew that.

I wondered if I'd ever understand Mike burying her under Ethan's last name, and started to worry that even if I spent months with the items in the box, many things about this woman and the love she inspired would forever remain a mystery.

It was a little after five and people were leaving the grounds, probably going home to dinner or wherever they felt they could best overcome their grief. Cemeteries will always be sad places, with loved ones gone, leaving loved ones behind, and that cemetery was no different.

Something flashed ahead and hurt my eyes, like a mirror catching the light just right. I looked to see what it was and was once again stunned by how much love Zelda got from two distinctly different men. The flash came from the tombstone of the grave with flowers; the sun reflecting off Ethan's shiny I.D. tags. Mike must have cemented them to it as some sort of guardians of her grave.

The carving on the headstone answered so many of my questions, and for the second time that day I was jealous of another woman, this time Zelda. The stone simply read, *Zelda Ross, beloved wife of Mike Richards, who gives her in death what eluded her in life – the name of the man she loved.*

I couldn't remain standing, and steadied myself against the headstone as I felt my body fold onto the ground. My fingers traced the letters of her name, and then trembled along the rest of the stone. The dates of her short life were etched above a beautiful stand of bamboo with a glorious sunrise behind it. Almost hidden in the middle of the tangle of bamboo was a beautiful flower, a peace lily, and its symbolism was not lost on me. Mike must have understood that he took Zelda away by being her refuge, a peaceful if unfulfilling partner who never forced her to do the hard things necessary for her own good. He was the lily, but the bamboo showed that he never forgot that the peace he offered was surrounded and forever threatened by her love for Ethan.

I was a damned tough lady and had been for a long time, but as I realized how unfathomable the passion was between Zelda and Ethan, something inside me shattered. Something painful but at the same time liberating, a collection of things I desperately needed to lose and gain but didn't understand at all. I'd gone to Naples with doubts about the perfect love Ethan felt for Zelda, but I suddenly understood that its imperfections were exactly what made it so beautiful. His box of letters had cracked open my heart to the truth that I'd spent most of my life terrified, refusing to surrender to either of those two most basic human needs: to love or be loved. No wonder I was frightened to write about it.

I hid under my umbrella as I started to cry, for Ethan and Zelda, for Mike, and for all of us who never had anything close to their love. Mostly I cried for myself, for the chances I knew I would continue to avoid and the risks I would refuse to take. For the men I'd treated badly for no other reason than my expectation that they would someday do the same to me, and for the one man among them who might have found me lovable, but had since moved on and forgotten our paths ever crossed.

It was long past dusk before I managed to stop my tears and the shaking of my body, yet even then I was unable to stop what I felt. I hoped to do better back in my car. I knew I could compartmentalize this if I tried hard enough. I could endure anything. I could endure everything. I would not let this feeling overwhelm me. I could not yield to it because it was far too scary.

The cemetery was nearly empty. A worker was waiting patiently for the last few people to leave so he could close the gate. As I walked toward my car I saw a well-dressed black man with a ponytail in the nearby shadows, holding a cluster of flowers and watching me closely. He was sobbing.

CHAPTER 15 - The Courage to Write

My mother paints. I would never have guessed that. She cautiously showed me some of her work after dinner that night of my return while my father stood proudly in the background, a role I remember him playing well and happily when I performed ballet or acted on stage or did any of the things parents watch their small children do.

Her paintings are abstracts, and as such to be interpreted under the influence of whatever the observer brings to them. At least that's what I've always heard. I think many people would see colorful flowers against a midnight sky in her paintings, as improbable as that sounds. But what I see in the splashes of light and threatening dark colors is her suffering, her goodness and innocence abused by the swirls of allegations that very nearly destroyed her life, and would certainly have done so if she hadn't set her jaw so determinedly. Her paintings, I'm ashamed to believe, were where she grieved for what I'd taken away from my parents' lives. Of course, that being nothing more than my own interpretation leaves room for me to be wrong,

197

and to hope that I am. I'm anxious to see what she might paint next.

I was late getting back to the city after visiting them, but I wasn't tired. I was happy and actually a little euphoric.

It's funny that I'd never applied that word to myself before.

I slept well, better than I can remember ever sleeping. As impossible as it seemed, I'd actually been forgiven for doing such a horrible thing to them. It wasn't even that difficult for my parents, and that made me realize the love I'd missed for so long was always there. I just hadn't allowed myself to see it. To do so would have required me to also see the terrible damage I'd done. No one would want to see that, and so I'd abandoned my own hope of love in order to avoid the love my parents had for me, and the guilt for my vengeful lie.

What was even more incredible was that I was actually accepting the idea of forgiving myself. That was unbelievably hard, and every minute of the day I wanted to backslide. All that afternoon I said more times than I could remember, "Molly, give yourself a break. You screwed up, but it's time to forgive." I expected to say it hundreds more times over the following days, but less the next week, I hoped, and less the week after that. I would get there, and soon.

I was clacking away at the keyboard like a woman possessed, but so far I'd just copied the notes Ethan wrote on his letters that last night in his empty home. They were his words, not mine, so it was easy. The courage for *me* to write? I guessed I would know soon enough.

I made a good step in the right direction by promoting my secretary, Heather, to an associates position so I could stay home mornings and at least try to write. In doing so I, Molly Edwards, made her so happy she jumped in the air. I couldn't believe it, and don't remember ever before touching someone that powerfully. She caught me up so entirely in her enthusiasm that we actually laughed together. I took her out to dinner, and while we ate I confessed that I'd always wanted to write, and only became an agent to be near the craft. "I took on this book," I said, "as my chance to see if I can do it."

"You'll be great, Molly. I just know you will."

It was nice of her to think so.

I put the picture of Ethan and Zelda beside my computer screen. I loved looking at it while I wrote, and did so all the time. I put it in a funny frame I shopped hard to find, one that had "Love Ain't For Sissies" laser-engraved on the wood. She's got her arm draped around his neck and he's pressing into her. Her dress is low-cut and sexy and she is absolutely beautiful. They both are. I'd finally realized that it came from the inside out.

In spite of its monetary value, I'd burned the hideous picture that Jonathan painted of me suffering at Zelda's grave, the one that made me vomit when he gave it to me in his studio. That war within me was finally over, thank God, and there was reason to celebrate gloriously and unashamed on my own style of canvas – this manuscript.

On the wall beside me I hung a litho of his painting of bamboo that their daughters donated to the museum. I looked at it when I needed inspiration, at the stand of bamboo bending to the wind and rain, taking the harsh punishment but not quite beaten by it. In my mind I imagined a hurricane was powering the wind, the same hurricane that roared into Nassau the night Ethan sailed out to sea.

When I was down in Naples the first time for research, I'd lied to the owner of Ethan's house. Not because I enjoyed being a liar, but because I didn't even allow myself to believe in Ethan's death until I understood it. I had to know why a man cherished by so many people would kill himself so pointlessly. As I flew home from that first trip to Naples, trying to ignore the internal battle that started spontaneously at Zelda's grave – a battle that came to head months later in Jonathan's studio – I was finally able to understand the truth. Ethan tried to explain it before, when I gave my reasons for not taking a chance on that rare occasion when a man might ask me out, but I guess I just wasn't listening.

"There's a recklessness to love," he said, "a willingness to abandon everything safe to pursue what's pure. Take a chance, Molly. Be reckless."

Ethan's unshakeable devotion to Zelda inspired the most powerful lesson of my life, and by writing these last few paragraphs I am trying very hard to be reckless. It is so out of character for the person I've been for so long that I'm terrified. I feel absolutely vulnerable, but I also feel as free as I did at my parents' home, liberated in a clean and honest sort of way as I evolve slowly toward the person I want so desperately to become. Of course it's uncomfortable, but it gets less so with each word I type and reckless thing I do.

Yesterday I smiled back at a man at the deli. He was much older than me and kind looking, so it was a pretty safe move that still, somehow, felt risky.

Last evening I told someone I didn't know how nice he looked. We were waiting to cross a street and he caught me looking at him. My first reaction was to challenge where he was looking, but instead "Good looking suit. Watch the puddle" came out. He said, "If you like the suit, then I'm very glad I chose it."

I thought about that all last night when I should have been reading submissions. As I sat at my desk I realized I've always looked for the bad in people, and I've always managed to find it. Now I'm in awe of how easily people return a smile and a kindness. How anxious people are to be nice. How good we are by nature.

I'm ashamed of how long it took me to learn this.

I called the publisher's office this morning and got the name of the receptionist who has always feared me. Bob. What an easy name. How hard would it have been for me to remember a nice, helpful guy named Bob.

This morning, as I dropped off the final outline of this manuscript for Rudy, I gave Bob a potted sprout of the bamboo from Ethan's estate. He was shocked. I thought he'd be suspicious after all the times I've snubbed him (I'm glad it hurts me to admit that), but he didn't seem to be. He stood, and then somehow managed to stammer his way through an invitation for lunch to repay. I'm still dumbfounded by the way he looked at me, and still feeling good about it. He's young and sweet and clearly just being nice, but we're meeting for hamburgers tomorrow and I'm excited. Isn't that cute? Hamburgers.

I spent today's lunch shopping for a new outfit. For a lark I tried on one of the pretty spring dresses just hitting the stores. In the dressing room I looked cute, and I loved seeing myself that way again. The hem billowed out when I swirled around, sexy in the most innocent of ways. I giggled and didn't want to take it off. Although I'm frightened of wearing something so fun again, I'm also anxious and can hardly wait. No one in New York has ever seen me in anything that wasn't severe or plain or both.

Kind of a shame, I think.

No, I'm not kidding myself. I know I've only made tiny steps toward what I now want, especially compared to the wild sacrifices Ethan would make. But they *are* steps. Recklessness does not come easily to me. To be honest, I lost two night's sleep worrying about admitting to the dress.

Sometimes I'll see a special couple, the kind that broadcasts their passion just by the way they hold hands, and I'm always tempted to ask if they know anything about bamboo, all the while looking into their eyes for a beautiful admission that I'd found Ethan and Zelda in their next life. For some reason that seems entirely possible to me now, even as I drag around the cynical vestiges of the *old* me that would never believe such foolishness.

But I don't ask, mostly because I've rarely seen two people who share what Ethan had with Zelda or, I guess, my dad has with Mom. I'm not giving up though, because thanks to them I do believe it's out there. I just need to keep being reckless to find it.

Like Ethan. I finally understand that he lived a glorious life that sent ripples through hundreds of others. But I still couldn't understand his death, at least not until this morning. As I typed the hand scrawled notes he'd written on his letters to Zelda after closing down their home, I was shattered to recognize a line he would use again in his very last e-mail on the night he sailed out of Nassau. I'd read it dozens of times without catching the significance, but his words finally made sense, and made his sailing into the blackness of a nighttime hurricane the most natural thing in this or any other world.

Even though I knew Zelda belonged with me instead of Mike, I'd promised God and myself never to damage another man's marriage, and I took that vow seriously. But given any righteous chance at all, I'd chase her to heaven or hell without a moment's hesitation.

Ethan, I truly do hope you found Zelda in the storm that night.

My love and thanks to you both – Molly

CHAPTER 16 - Appendix

The story of Ethan and Zelda's love both ends and begins with their deaths. As the screenwriter and I talked about the ending he said, "We'll wrap by rerunning twenty seconds of footage from the very beginning, where Ethan and you were both holding the box and your hands faded out on his last night in Naples. Remember? Then once again we'll elevate the camera, looking down. But this time we'll rise through the ceiling of Ethan's empty house and way up into the sky so that the audience gets a shot of the sun, far off and low on an horizon. I'll leave it to each individual viewer to decide if it's rising or setting as the camera closes in on the horizon until Ethan's shipwrecked sailboat – terribly beaten from the hurricane – comes into view on the deserted beach in the distance. Swell the music, fade out, roll credits."

I like his idea for the ending. Frank is an artist, I think, and not just a screenwriter.

What follows is supplemental material to this book. Read it, don't read it, the choice is yours. They are a few of the actual letters from the box Ethan sent me. I haven't changed any words, and only typed them because Ethan's handwriting is nearly illegible. If I hadn't, the notes he made on his last night in Naples would have remained a mystery to all but the handful of us who can decipher it.

The publisher only allowed me a few pages for letters so I chose the ones that made the most impact on me. I omitted some because they played so heavily on my mind that they worked their way into this story. *Making Love*, for instance, came from a letter Ethan wrote to his closest friend, who allowed me to use it in this book. Other letters were too personal to include.

I left out one letter in pure defiance of Ethan, a letter of apology he wrote to Zelda's first husband, Paul. Ethan asked me to include "the parts I'm proud of and the parts that still shame me," but I refuse to do it. I can't agree with the angst Ethan felt over their divorce. Marriages break up everyday and there's always a reason, possibly nothing more than the fact that they're destined to fail. Personally, I think he held himself to too high a standard, but I'm not surprised. It kind of falls in line with the way he lived, and the way he died. – M.E.

ETHAN'S LETTER TO ZELDA'S FATHER

Dear Martin:

I'm sure I surprised you the other night, and so I'm writing this letter to confirm what I said and to reassure you that I've spent two years pondering what to do. I know Zelda's sickness can easily throw her off balance, and have read dozens of books about the challenges presented by manic-depression. Yet I have decided to not only pursue her, but to also pursue the mission of helping her through those dark and scary occasions when she'll need me most. My love will make it easy, and besides, it's a chance to make some small repayment for her civilizing me.

Not that I was ever uncivilized, but I lived as if everyone's life depended on my strength and speed and skill. That kind of bladed mentality takes its toll on a person, and Zelda showed I could put it all behind me. I cannot yet say that I've beaten my sword into a plowshare, but I will proudly admit to having allowed dust to gather on the glistening blade as it sits unused in my closet. I am forever thankful your daughter showed me how to do that.

I have seen her depressed, by the way, so don't worry that I'm unaware and therefore might run when trouble strikes. I had no idea what was happening the first time, when Paul was out of town and she wrecked her car. She called me so hysterical and full of grief I was barely able to make sense of her words. It took hours to calm her down, and I did it clumsily, but I do believe I helped. I have since built upon that experience. You understand better than me how those helping skills are learned. Little by little and experience by experience.

I also see clearly the wonderful side to her craziness, when she's zany and fun and self-deprecating in so fearless a way. At those times – which are by far the majority – she is a delight without equal. The world sees her that way most of the time, which is why everyone loves her so much.

Martin, I understand that as with most things in life, Zelda's not perfect. It's just damned hard for me to see her imperfections. You should know I intend to retain my poor vision in that regard as I ask your support in my fight to take her away from Paul. If necessary I will work against you as I would an enemy, but I know you see what we have, and pray you will not require that of me.

Sincerely, Ethan Ross

(Below I've typed what Ethan scribbled below the letter on his last night in the States)

Molly,

It's almost eight and I should be dressed, but I can't seem to put this stuff down and get moving toward my going away party.

My daughters came by an hour ago to take Smudge. It was a sad time, them hugging me and then walking out to their car with my cat and her things in their arms. They didn't look like the beautiful young women they've become. They looked like my little girls. That's the way I'll remember them, their softness and love overwhelming me.

It was only last week I told them I was leaving. We were out at dinner and had our usual great time, teasing each other and playing liar's poker while we waited for the food. Then they asked how I was doing since Zelda left and I said, "Not too well. Thinking about leaving the country. You two okay with that?"

They normally would have been, I know. I've raised them to be independent women and they understand what that means in terms of what they do with their lives, and how much they depend on me to do for them. I take good care of them, I think, but I'm most proud of teaching them how to take good care of themselves.

Even though they've watched me leave and return so many times from so many countries that it no longer fazes them, what did worry them this evening was my heart. – ER

A WALK ON A PIER

The following two letters are included with permission from Zelda's father. When I went to his Washington office I was sure he would say no, that the fear of social and political fallout would make it too unwise and too costly to allow his daughter's sickness and divorce – family matters – to be so widely exposed. But instead he stared at a picture of Zelda as a little girl on the beach. He looked like he still didn't believe she'd died. Then he asked, "Did you ever meet my daughter?"

I said that I had, and that I thought she was adorable, just like everyone else seemed to feel. He smiled at me and said, "I'm very proud of her. She was amazingly happy with Ethan, so I guess I'm proud of myself too." Then, as his appointments secretary signaled my need to leave, he rose and said, "I'd be pleased to have my letter to her included in your book, as well as my note to Ethan. Even with the way it turned out, I don't have the slightest regret over what I did."

Only one other time have I been so impressed with a man as a father. – M.E.

Dear Ethan:

In my role as Zelda's father I take seriously any threat to her happiness. Therefore you can understand that the letter you wrote has caused more than a few sleepless nights. Although I've never blinded myself to the challenges of her marriage to Paul, it is a marriage. You should not have lost sight of that.

I've seen you many times over the last few years when we've come down from New England to vacation. Janet and I have always liked you, Ethan, and have enjoyed seeing the way you interact with our daughter. When you two are together it's as if you were children, and I'm not sure I've ever seen anything so delightful as the way she acts around you. I'll never forget her chasing you around the party store on our last day there. She was so determined to tickle you and you were just as determined not to let her. I thought we would all hurt ourselves laughing, not only at your antics, but at the stunned face of the old woman when she realized the hooligans zipping through the aisles were fully grown adults. She would have talked for hours in the parking lot about the love she saw in you two.

Ethan, have you thought about the impact on Zelda's life if you pursue her? I can't stop you, but if you love her the way you say you do, don't you worry for her? She's safe with Paul. Perhaps she's not as happy or loved as I would like, but she is safe. Paul is a good provider and always will be. You've assured me you'll do an even better job, and that requires me to ask if you really understand the challenge you seek. You say you're aware that she has an illness that can lead

209

her to deep states of depression, but do you know how damaging and hurtful she can be at those times? I do. I've been there when both she and her mother have gone through it. It's hard and painful work, requiring an incredible amount of love and twice that much patience. Be sure you're up for this task that, on occasion, will have hateful things hurled your way.

Ethan, you have succeeded in doing something my political rivals would envy by putting me in a tough position I cannot ignore: should I support what you want and encourage the destruction of my daughter's marriage? Tell her she belongs in your arms and trust you to make her happy? Or should I do what's safest and quite possibly best: tell her to avoid you and focus on Paul. Having seen you together leaves no doubt you two have something amazing and pure, but still it's a very tough choice you've given me. I hope you know how hard the decision was.

Along with this note I'm sending back a copy of the letter you wrote me, not only to help you remember your vow, but to let you see what I wrote on it before putting it in the mail it to Zelda. Because you've played straight with me I want to do the same.

My Dearest Daughter,

I'm making this note on Ethan's letter because you might as well have all the facts at once. I hope you can deal with this, but if not you can always come home or I'll fly down there. Don't hesitate to call. I can be there in a few hours.

Just before your mom and I came back from Naples we all went down to the pier, remember?

210

You and Mom and the kids walked ahead while Ethan and I lagged behind, engaged in one of those terrific conversations I always seem to have with him. Paul was, as usual, at work.

About half way to the end Ethan stopped, looked me straight in the eyes, and said, "Martin, I want you to know I'm in love with your daughter."

I think he kept talking after that but I wasn't sure. A father doesn't hear those kinds of things very often, and I confess that a part of me was instantly happy because I know you're not quite content with Paul. Even so, I wanted him to take back his words and promise never to repeat them.

"I've loved her since I first saw her," he was saying when I got back my senses. "I want you to know I intend to marry her someday. I don't mind waiting and I don't mind suffering while I do. I've tried to hide my love but I'm sure she knows, and as her father I want you to be certain of my intentions."

Little Girl, you and I have never been close, and although I'm not sure of the reason, I am sure that I've always loved you. Perhaps the problem was mine in that the world adored you so much. Maybe I felt I was in a competition I had no chance of winning, and therefore chose to focus on the political campaigns I knew I could win. Maybe I felt resentment or guilt for your depression, or maybe I avoided you to make your recovery easier, knowing how hard it was for you to come out of that dark tunnel knowing you'd said bad things to me and other people who loved you.

Or maybe I was just too worn out by your mom's same sickness to give you the patience, love, and attention you deserved. For all of that, there's surely a part of you that resents me, and believe me, I understand.

I received this letter from Ethan after we got back to New England. He's put me in a position I cannot ignore, and I feel like your entire future hinges on what I say, all the hopes and dreams I have for you.

If you love him back – and I already know the answer to that – there are huge challenges ahead for the two of you. I'm frightened they may overwhelm you, that they'll present too many hardships for someone so innocent. And to be totally honest, I'm scared you'll have a relapse and end up back in a hospital. I've seen it happen several times with your mother. It doesn't take a big problem to trigger it either, and the possibility always exists that you could go in and never come out.

My darling little girl, after more quiet walks, chewed fingernails, and late nights praying than I've had in decades, I've decided to see Ethan as an opportunity, and his uncomfortable proposal a gift, a chance to do something incredibly hard and defining for my precious daughter. By defying the rules of a society I've lived my life accommodating, perhaps I can finally prove how much I love you.

So with a hand that trembles I write these words: Go to him, Honey, and live happily. I've never seen a better match in my entire life, and I feel lucky and proud you've found so intense a love.

212

Adoringly, Daddy

RUN THROUGH THE JUNGLE

Dear Triple-Sexy-Gorgeous,

I know I'm running a risk mailing this to you, even though I'm sending it through Bill. Destroy it after you read it, or send it to someone else for safekeeping. There's no reason to cause a problem on the home front.

I got here okay and have a day before slipping into the jungle to cross the border. I'm doing fine and everything's working out; a couple of smugglers have agreed to let me come along. It was lucky for me we had a mutual contact from Nicaragua. None of us knew him well, but just knowing who he was and what he did built enough trust between us. We leave tomorrow night after the curfew. Should be interesting.

I miss you so much. I'm going to be very lonely for the next few weeks, but that loneliness will only heighten the thrill of seeing you again. What's the old line, "Being lost is worth the coming home?" I've always loved the travel and adventure of my life, but you've somehow made it seem appealing to stay put. How and when did you manage to do that? I never even noticed.

When I boarded my plane in Miami a white-haired old man wheeled his wife onboard. An attendant tried to help but the old boy just smiled as if to say, "Thanks, but she's my wife and I'm damn proud to take care of her."

I could see in their eyes that these two people had what we have. This is the first time I've said that, even with all the people I meet. Up until that

213

day I could have easily believed the kind of love they showed belonged to you and me alone.

They were two rows ahead of me and across the aisle, and as he bent down to buckle her seatbelt he looked up at me. I winked and smiled and he did the same. He kissed her cheek, and then walked past me to get her a blanket. As he returned he put his hand on my shoulder and squeezed. It was as if he had seen in my eyes that I too love a woman that much, that my entire heart and being belong to someone like his wife, the perfect woman I was lucky enough to find.

I am so thankful for Paul's travels that allow me the chance to nurse you when you're sick, rescue you when you need it, and help with a hundred chores and events that would have been mundane except for our being together. You've done the same and more for me, helping me heal both mentally and physically and showing me that what I really wanted, besides you, was to be the best person I could possibly be, a helper instead of a warrior in this screwed-up world. Even now, I hope this incursion enables me to help some of these people, regardless of who's right or wrong politically.

It was nice to see the old man and woman carrying such an intense love so close to the grave. Those two sweet people convinced me they'll carry their love beyond this life, and that's really what I want to say to you, the reason I decided to risk writing. Our love won't ever end. I know you worry that something will happen to me somewhere in the world, and even though the places I go aren't nearly as dangerous as you think, life is always a risk, even back in the

States. If I die, I want you to have absolute confidence that I'm not leaving you. I'll always be with you, and then one day far off you'll die and we'll be together again, most likely finding each other in our next life the way we feel we've done through the ages. What we have is too beautiful not to survive.

I still have to buy some used clothing so I don't stand out so much, but I have a few more minutes and want to keep writing. I feel so close to you, even this far away. I know you're thinking of me. I hope you're not feeling guilty. You love me and I love you and we can't help that. We've admitted it to each other but that's all we've done. I know we both feel guilty about Paul, but as long as nothing physical passes between us I think I can live with my conscience. I'm not sure, but for you I'll run the risk.

I am so incredibly proud of you for applying for that job with Van's firm. I'm sorry I had to leave without finding out how it went. I know you were terrified of the interview, and I quite honestly didn't think you'd do it. Did you wear the dress I suggested? Use any of the lines we rehearsed? Doesn't matter; I'm sure you did wonderfully. I'd call Van and ask what he thought, but I don't want to meddle and wouldn't call from here anyway.

If you get this job I want you to know you did it on your own. Don't credit me with it the way you always give credit to others. You should be singularly proud of yourself. You plucked up the courage to go without a resume or corporate experience, and I could not possibly be more impressed.

Don't worry about the pay. Whatever they offer will be fine because you're not there for the money. You've told me often how much you doubt your worth, and I believe that most of those doubts will disappear once you start getting recognized as the valuable employee I'm sure you'll become. You will eventually have enough raises and commendations to outweigh any doubts you grew up with, and at that point you'll quit and go back to art full time. The bold step you've just made will change your life. I wouldn't be surprised if future sculptures reflect those changes. Again, I am so proud of you.

All my love, Fitz

Writer's Note: I find it interesting that by my best guess Ethan writes this letter to Zelda only a year or so after meeting her. I would have loved to ask him about that, but as with so many of his secrets – what he really did for a living besides writing; how he knew so many facts I could never uncover; and why he had sources all over the world – I suppose the actual time their relationship started will remain another one of his mysteries – M.E.

THINGS I LOVE ABOUT ZELDA

The way she smiles and asks "Kay?" when she's pushing me into something

Her whine for a latte in bed on weekend mornings, followed by a wonderful kiss and lots of excitement when I bring it

The loyalty and love that automatically makes her assume that whoever opposes me about anything must be wrong

Her initial step when she first begins to walk, which looks like she's stepping off a ledge

Her ability to smile and be happy in the midst of incredible turmoil

Her courage to fight her sickness, coupled with the courage to hide it from others

The way she smiles knowingly as she asks things from people, as if expecting to get her way even though she's really full of doubt

Her endless questions that make us spend three nights watching a two hour movie

Gosh, Molly, it was fun reading this. I wrote it about three years into our relationship, and all I remember is that we'd had some stupid fight the night before and she shot me some line like, "I don't know what you see in me that makes you stay."

I came home and dashed off this list, and then at about two in the morning I cut a rose from my garden, clipped off the thorns, and drove back to her condo. She was so adorable when she slept, so tiny and fragile. I worried about her all the time, and the times she slept were no exception. It seemed that Zelda's life and sanity were always threatened. She was small and trusting and therefore vulnerable to the world around her, but she was even more helpless and vulnerable to the world inside her head, a world that went along with her most of the time but occasionally dragged her in some utterly sad or incredibly joyous direction.

I always wanted to be there to share in that joy or help her through that sadness, and somewhere along the line that became my mission. I reveled in it, and dedicated myself to creating an environment where she could live fully and still be safe.

And it was this wonderful, zany, sometimes tragic part of Zelda that helped in my discovery of a good part of me. Some people would say she was sick, I guess, but I would never say that because she was my teacher. She was sick because I needed her to be, much the same way she needed me to be strong. Her illness inspired me to read psychology books and study clinical cases, talk to professionals and learn how to help her. She never wanted to admit that she took medication, or that the medication occasionally failed, and it happened so seldom I can understand why. Yet someone needed to help her when the sobbing and desperation started, and I cherished that role. By helping her, I helped myself realize how selfish I'd been, surprising me with how small a human being I was before I met her.

I put the note and the rose on the pillow beside her and then kissed her softly. Very gently I straightened the sheets over her, and left. The next morning I was working at my desk when I heard my front door open. I stood up as she came in crying like a little girl. She walked up so quickly we almost fell when she collided into me. The list I'd written was all crumbled and soggy in one hand that dangled lifelessly toward the floor. The rose drooped from the other.

"This is the sweetest thing anyone's ever done for me."

I put my arms around her and buried her into my chest.

She sniffled and scraped her nose on my shirt as she moved her head up and down. "I love you so much."

What I would give to have that woman back. Not the woman who just left me to marry Mike, but the woman who cried over so simple a gesture.

Only now, Molly, do I realize that I was the one who destroyed her. I took that innocent, gentle woman and urged her toward independence and a career, always with a foolish confidence that I knew best for her. Sitting here alone in such an empty house, I can't believe I did it. What was I thinking?

Who was I to trust so fully that she needed to pursue the most accomplished life possible? I tried to create opportunities for her to do that, willing to spend whatever time and money necessary to make her happy. I was a man on a mission.

Why couldn't I see that once she had me, she already was happy?

Stupid, stupid me. – ER

LETTERS FROM ZELDA

Below I've combined several excerpts of the many letters Zelda wrote to Ethan. I'm fairly certain she never intended to send them, and I know there were some she never did. They were stacked and unfolded in the box Ethan sent as if she'd saved them for years, and then gave them to him at the same time she gave him the dress he loved.

I understand how Ethan's need for adventure scared Zelda because it did the same thing to me. Whenever he finished a book or had a lull in his writing – and sometimes when I needed him chained to his keyboard – he would take off without a word of warning for "a dose of adventure." My suspicion was that he used his extensive government training to freelance for the private army companies I've read about in the news, like the one whose contractors were hung off a bridge in Fallujah, Iraq, but that's just a guess. I never realized as I worried about his life and health that Zelda and I shared the same fear of his death. I *think* I wish I'd known, although I'm not sure it would have been any more comforting to worry together.

It seems to me that Zelda was the purest form of herself in her letters, when Ethan wasn't around to support her. Sometimes I read her letters in my office and sometimes alone in bed, getting to know her almost intimately and feeling the emotions about which she was writing. I wanted to be faithful in merging them, leaving out repetitions (her constant regret over her condition and the problems it caused), but preserving her simple statements that proved the love she felt for him.

Over the years that I've been an agent, hundreds of writers have sent me love stories, but none were as beautifully patient and wonderfully trusting as Zelda so simply and honestly writes. When I first set out on this project, all I knew was that Ethan loved this woman more completely than anything my own experience allowed me to understand, and so I assumed from his devotion that they had the kind of fairy-tale match I'd read about as a girl.

I was surprised to discover how wrong I was. For all of their love, Ethan and Zelda were far from immune to the hurts and jealousies that come with relationships. They had the same fights and vexing problems that most couples had, but what set them so far apart was their unshakeable faith that they would always be together. – M.E.

Dear Mr. Fluffy,

I can't believe you've gone away again. I'm happy because I know how you love an adventure, but I can't wait for you to come back to me. I'm going to have strawberries and wine and be *ready* when you return. You know what that means, tee-hee.

Ethan, the way you live thrills me. It makes you exciting to be around and, (this is more important) you're just as passionate with me. That feels wonderful. The way you are drives you to make our relationship the best possible.

But it also scares me that you do such wild things. If you got badly hurt, I don't know what I would do. If you got killed, I know exactly what I would do. Please, please, please be careful.

We have our share of fights, Ethan, and I swear I'm going to keep working on that. But there's magic in our relationship. I feel it most when talking, making love, and dancing with you.

Speaking of dancing, my friends are taking me to Ryan's Roadhouse this weekend. Remember all those great nights there? As soon as the band started I would drag you onto the dance floor because I couldn't wait. People loved seeing us together. It always felt like we gave them something they needed. Remember when that man and his wife sent us drinks to congratulate us. He figured we must be celebrating an engagement or something. They acted so funny when you said we'd been together much longer than them. They looked at each other like, "Well why aren't *we* like that?"

* * *

I love that you always focus on me when we talk. If I interrupt your work, you always turn away from it and listen to me. I know how hard that is. I can see in your eyes it's a very conscious decision. It's like you say to yourself, "Yes, my writing's important. I need to get these words on paper while they're fresh in my mind. But where are my priorities? With Zelda, of course." I might yak for quite a while, but you never make me feel rushed. Especially if I'm upset about something. I always feel like the very center of your world, and that's so nice. Do I do that to you, too? I hope so.

* * *

I don't even know where to mail this, Ethan, and probably never will, but I feel closer to you by writing. Since you'll probably never read this letter I'm going to say some things I might not say in person. But not because I don't think I could. There's just no easy answer. And I don't want to hurt you more than I already do. I understand why we haven't married yet, and I know we will, as soon as you're sure of my reasons for being with you. We both regret the time it's taken, but we'll get there.

You know what I noticed today? How empty the hours felt without hearing your voice. It means so much when you call work just to say hello and check on me. No matter how busy I am, when my secretary says, "Ethan is on the line," I smile.

I didn't know I needed that kind of attention until I got it. Now it's essential. The phone calls, notes, flowers, messages – you do them so naturally. Even after all this time. When you come back I'm going to do the same, and you're going to love it. Being a man doesn't make you different. You don't fool me with the toughness you show the world. You're soft as cotton inside. I've seen you cry too many times.

* * *

I thought I loved Paul, and I am sorry I took so long getting out. That's something I'd change if I could. I was foolish and scared. Paul was a decent man and I didn't want to hurt him. And then you and I both screwed up by hiding our love. I'm almost glad you got hurt and spent all that time in the hospital. Otherwise, who knows how long we would have gone on like that?

I've never lived alone until now, but even today, just these long hours alone show how you felt for almost three years of waiting. You didn't think I'd ever leave Paul. My actions didn't give you much hope.

Even so, I can never forgive you for what you did with Faith. And whether you know it or not, that's at the center of every single fight we have. Regardless of what starts it, I always end up going to thoughts of you and her together. That's why I get so mad. I'm still so hurt.

I understand how it happened. But from the time you left your wife, I've always known you'd be mine. You used to come to Paul's and my house and work so hard at hiding your love, but I knew you'd fallen for me.

You'll never be pure again, Ethan. I know you wouldn't have done it if I'd been with you, but I am so angry with you for staining your pureness. And I worry that the anger will never go so far away that it won't come back when I'm sick. You know I don't want it to. And I'm scared I might lose you over it. The way I keep reliving it. I love you, Ethan, and don't want that to happen. You have to help me get past it. I don't know how it's possible, but you've made all the other problems go away. So I know you can.

* * *

You're so faithful to me when we fight. I swear I don't know where those hateful words come from. I love you most when you stay with me while my demon inside takes it out on you.

Isn't it weird that the times I love you most are when I'm being meanest to you. Because I know that's when it's hardest for you to stay. Most men wouldn't. It's easy to love people who are easy. But you've proven you love me when it's pretty close to impossible. I've wondered why a lot. Do you feel sorry for me? Obliged to help? Are you just too good a man to walk out on someone in need?

What I finally decided is that you hate that side of me as much as I do. But you love the rest of me so much that you accept it. The good with the bad. The part that cherishes every inch of you most of the time. The part that can say horrible things to you.

You know how much I count on you when that happens. I have no idea what I might do if I couldn't. I am so comfortable knowing that nothing is more important than rescuing me. I've called you in meetings. Tennis matches. Movies. Not once have you done anything short of dropping everything in order to come help me. You've held me. Whispered to me. Saved me from the demon depression.

I love you so much Scotty – Z

ZELDA'S GOOD-BYE LETTER TO ETHAN

My Dearest Ethan,

We nearly got there, didn't we? Nine years of tough but incredibly good times.

We should have gotten married the first time we'd planned. Looking back, I'm not sure why I ran scared last January. I guess the reality caught up too suddenly with my dream. It felt like too good of a thing. Something I didn't deserve. I'll never understand it myself, so I can't explain it. But you probably don't need that. You're good at analyzing things. I argue with you about it, but I do think you understand me better than I do.

But what's happening now is different, I'm sure.

Ethan, I will always thank you for helping me grow as a person. Remember when we met, I didn't even know how to drive. Paul had me too dependent and doubt-riddled to learn. And you're the only person on this planet who saw that, and saw that I didn't work for the same reason. You knew how to help me, and why it was important. I acted like it didn't matter. But you knew the truth. Other than sculpting, I never thought I was smart enough to do anything worthwhile.

You always said I was far more capable than I believed. Never once did you lose faith in me. You pushed me to explore my life. To live it fully. That aggravated me a lot, but you were right. Look at me now. I know you're proud of me, even though I know you're disappointed I didn't move in with you. Or will be marrying you in March.

Our relationship has certainly been strange. All those years I stayed with Paul. Then all those years I wanted to move in. There was always a roadblock. Often it was something you wanted me to prove to myself. You never wanted me to feel undervalued and dependent again, like I did when I was married. I'm glad because you were right. I enjoy having my own career. I like knowing I can take care of myself.

Ethan, you must know that Mike loves me. I love him too. He is kind and sweet and we never fight about anything. He'll never take your place because he's not you, but that's both good and bad. Bad because of all the wonderful things I'll miss about you. Good because he looks at me without seeing the silly little woman you knew so well. The one who had a lay-in most mornings. Who had no choice but to whine sweetly when she needed help. Mike knows nothing of that woman. He only sees me for the success I am now. That feels good. Kind of like I've outrun a reputation I liked a lot but that no longer fits.

I've said before that I'm sorry I hurt you last year. You worked so hard to make your home comfortable for my children and me. Their rooms turned out beautifully. They loved the furniture and decorations and were sad when I told them it wasn't going to happen.

Now I have to apologize for hurting you almost a year to the day later. I shouldn't have called you in September. If I hadn't, we would never have gotten back together. I know you wouldn't have called me because I'd asked you not to. And you always respect my decisions. I still can't say whether the call was selfishness or love on my part.

Like you, I really wanted it to work between us. But being engaged to Mike has proven that my happiness depends on a fresh start. Just as you showed me how to make a fresh start all those years ago. Am I thanking you and blaming you at the same time? Maybe I am.

Anyway, I love you Ethan. I always will. You've done more for my life than everyone else combined. I will always adore you for that. Your love and faith and encouragement were more than any woman has a right to expect.

Tell you what: why don't we keep watching sunrises together? That's always been special to us, and I want to hold onto some of what we had together. It was incredible, for sure. I'll never find it again and neither will you. We were so lucky to have it once. We shouldn't regret that it didn't last.

So is it a deal? I'll look east each morning and watch the sun come up. You do it too, Sweetie. I guess I'll have to make my own coffee, but I promise you this, Ethan. When my lips touch the cup it will be a kiss meant for you. No one else will ever know. Our secret love, just the way we began.

I love you, Ethan. If I live a dozen more lives, I'll never find another man who wants so much good for me. Unless, of course, I find you in one of those lives.

To sunrises, my dear, dear man ... Z

ETHAN'S GOOD-BYE TO ZELDA

My Beautiful Zelda,

I remember so clearly the moment we met. I'd found your drivers license and rode my bike over to return it. I was sweaty and probably stinky but when I saw you something changed inside me, as if a part of me I didn't know existed had just sprung to life. I know it happened to you too.

228

You were amazing back then. You still are, but in a different way for which I'll take the blame. I know you're proud of yourself, and thankful for my help, but I tell you truthfully you were better when we first met. Successful business people aren't rare. Innocent and happy people are. Back then, all you ever wanted were little victories, particularly if they made others happy. You had a childlike quality I should have cherished instead of leading you to a career that now comes ahead of your health and those who love you.

I pray that the changes in you are temporary, and that one day you'll hang up your suits and go back to being the wonderful, silly gift you once were to the world. For the first three years of our relationship you were a blinding burst of color and inspiration to me, and so that's all I plan to take forward in my memory – the most beautiful flowers of the garden we grew together.

Zelda, I don't want to stick around Naples to see the end, reading about you and Mike in the papers, so I'll say good-bye now and close our book before reading that last and painful page. I know you think you've read it already, but I don't want to. I want to wonder about the future. Will you really marry Mike? I'm guessing you will. Will you be happy? I don't know. You and I were a blue-flame rocket ride, and I think you want and need the excitement of a relationship like ours. Perhaps I do too. It was stimulating and fantastic in a way most couldn't comprehend, but by God there was never anything boring about us.

I think you'll find Mike boring. If so, will you be so disoriented that you'll leave him and your career and look for me somewhere? Who knows, life is nothing if not unpredictable.

So there we have it, I guess. The end, at least for now. For my part the ending of our relationship will never be written, like the story F. Scott Fitzgerald was working on when he died. Who knows how it was really intended to wind up?

You've heard, I'm sure, that I sold this home and land I love so much. It was fairly easy once you were no longer here. Only two things made the sale difficult. One was the giant bamboo Jonathan gave us. I can't believe how tall and beautiful it grew, towering above the surrounding palm trees.

The other thing I hate to leave is our garden. Your watermelons are growing well. The carrots are small and we planted the corn too late, although there are some cute, small ears on them. We didn't know anything about growing vegetables, but wasn't that a nice weekend – turning over the earth, planting the seeds, labeling the rows? If we'd survived we would have planted earlier next year to account for the Florida season.

I bought a sailboat, similar to the one I had years ago that I showed you in pictures, and not much different than the one in the story I wrote you at our beginning. I named this boat *Waiting* too, because that's kind of what I'll be doing. I'm leaving tomorrow and cannot guess at the circumstances under which I might see you again, and for that reason I'm including my agent's phone number and address. If you ever want to find me, she'll tell you how to get in touch. If you ever need any money, I've instructed her to draw off the royalties she's holding for me and give you whatever you need.

I will kiss you back in the mornings.

With all the love I've ever had for a woman ... to sunrises, Ethan

THE REST OF THE LETTER ETHAN WROTE TO ACCOMPANY THE BOX

February 20, 1995

Hey, Molly,

So there you have it, the whole story of Zelda and me, the parts I've kept private because I love them so much or regret them even more. You've always wondered about the magic that kept her and me so thrilled with such a difficult relationship, so maybe these letters will provide some insight. I don't know. My own vision is clouded by proximity because I'm so close to her and the past. I'll always live in it, a relic from some other and more beautiful time who will forever be out of touch with the real world. Nine years together did nothing to diminish my excitement, and everything to heighten it. Her eyes never lost their grip, and the touch of her hand was far more exciting at the end than the beginning. The sound of her voice always made me smile, no matter how many times a day I heard it. How is that possible?

Losing someone I love that much could never make me stop loving her. However it will keep me from loving again. It wouldn't be fair to another woman. Zelda was the one woman I was meant to find, the greatest gift of my life. All I had to do was accept her as she was, instead of

231

wanting her life to be the best it could possibly be, at least according to my ideal. In giving her that, I lost her.

Maybe that's the way these things are supposed to work. Maybe I was just a guide to her, someone instrumental but temporary in her life. I guess I can accept that role, especially if I made a contribution that's made her happier.

Molly, now I'm going to stick my nose a little into your business, the kind of thing I rarely do. I don't get the impression you've ever been willing to risk being hurt and I guess I understand why: the reward seems false and certainly not worth the gamble.

As I read over Zelda's and my history and make a couple of notes about what I feel in my heart, I'd really like you to consider taking that chance. Even now, seeing how disappointingly this worked out, at least for now, I have no regrets. In fact, I feel quite opposite of that. I'm thrilled by the experience of having once been truly loved by someone I loved truly. I did a bad thing by breaking up another man's marriage. I sacrificed a good wife. I suffered years of loneliness waiting for her to be free. And you know what? The remnants alone, these little pieces and memories I carry with me, are worth far more than the price.

If you ever find someone you love, take the chance. Run the risk. Don't be afraid to be their prisoner. I am now and will forever be Zelda's. I would choose no other option.

I know you've felt sorry for me that I'm alone and so badly hurt. But the hurt started going away soon after she left me for Mike, and eventually, all that will remain are my good memories. I never expect to be alone out on the sea or in strange ports because in the calm of the evenings and the independence of my days, I'll feel her more strongly than I would with the interfering chaos of American society. Zelda's love will travel with me, Molly, and that means she will too. At least in my heart. And isn't that always the best part of any relationship?

Gosh, look at the time. I can't believe I killed the night doing this. If I still had a phone I'm sure it would have rung a dozen times, people asking when I'm coming to the party. I'll dash over there after I pack this up, and hope a few folks are still hanging around. They're good friends so I bet they stayed. I feel bad for making them wait.

I'll ask Brett to mail this box after he takes me to the marina tomorrow. You'll also find a copy of the good-bye letter I mailed to Zelda this afternoon, the one I told you about with your phone number on it. I'm thanking you in advance for being the contact should that day ever come.

Don't know when I'll write you again but I will be writing. I'll be safe so don't worry. Unless something goes wrong I expect my first port to be St. Thomas, so I'll call you from there. – ER

AN OLD LETTER FROM THE ISLANDS

(I include this last one because of the hope it gave me he would one day return)

March 23, 1998

Dear Molly,

Congratulations on the sale of my last novel. You negotiated excellent terms, so thanks. You'll be glad to know I'm making solid progress on the other book I mentioned, the one that deals with some of the work I did after leaving the FBI. Writing about the pain I inflicted, or had inflicted upon me, is a cathartic experience, one I feel slowing the swirl of violence that once infected me but that causes fewer problems each new day down here in the islands. When it sells, yes, I'll come to New York to meet with the publisher.

I picked up mail in Eleuthera and received five of your letters from the last four months, not counting my copy of the most recent publishing agreement. I can tell you're worried about me and want me to come home. My parents are worried too, and so are my children, but you must all trust that I'm fine. It's as if I'm living from the pages of a book, and I guess I enjoy it. I would certainly prefer the book to be turning out differently, but perhaps my life reflects my choices in literature. I have always been a sucker for a heart-breaking tragedy, especially when it brings to close a life of intense experiences.

I can also tell that you feel I've wasted all the years you've known me loving a woman who was never mine, but as I've probably said before, at the very outset of our time together I think I knew I'd never have Zelda. She and I were like partners from some other life, right down to the hard-to-understand fact that we both enjoyed tension in our relationship. She sure kept me wound up by flirting and teasing and keeping me on my toes a hundred percent of the time. I can't tell you how often I fell for it when we'd be making love and she'd "confess something." Not once did I have the confidence to laugh it off, but neither did I ever hear of any evidence she was unfaithful. It was just a game she played to keep my toes tingling, and as I said, it was powerful magic in our relationship.

Molly, I know you'll be happy to learn that I've recently been able to imagine returning to the States to live. It's still some years away, but I'd like to start some kind of a writing enclave. I've always wanted to teach college, but since I don't have an M.F.A. this would be a good alternative. I'll buy some land like I had before and build guest cottages on it. I'll sponsor a quarterly writing contest with a cheap fee even some talented but impoverished writer could afford to pay. The ten most inspired and honest writers will come to the enclave at my expense to push each other, and me most of all.

I'm happy to have that idea rolling around so heavily in my head. It's something I could love in my life, something that might hold some of the same excitement and challenge as loving Zelda. Keep it in mind, my friend.

Later, Gator … Ethan

About the Author

Wes is a real-life adventurer, one of those people who turns life on its head and shakes the change from its pockets. A global traveler, yacht rat, intellectual, surf bum, bow-hunter, actor, romantic, former F.B.I./S.W.A.T. Agent and Security Consultant, raconteur and all-around fun guy, Wes can debate Voltaire and Rousseau while wrenching on a greasy diesel far out at sea, or drop into a point break wave as skillfully as he's crept within grasp of wild game.

Over the past dozen years Wes (wesdemott.com) has garnered international acclaim for his novels about prisoners of war, the FBI, military assassins, and spies. In his beautiful but heartbreaking novel, *Loving Zelda*, he wrote about hope and loss and the chance to change our lives if we're fearless enough to try.

Tortuga Gold reflects a fun new chapter in Wes's own life as he's joined in his adventures by his beautiful Belgian wife, Sabine, a human rights/refugee lawyer who spent seven of her fifteen years with the United Nations living in Africa, including full-time residency in the war zones of Rwanda, Burundi, and the Congo during their bloody genocides.

Wes's love of the ocean often plays into his short stories and novels. He's boated thousands of miles on dozens of his own boats, surfed world famous breaks, and caught or speared game fish since he was thirteen. In 2010, after sailing from the Chesapeake Bay to Florida's West Coast and selling their home, Wes and Sabine made a permanent move aboard their new boat, a trawler they named *Wasafiri* ("The Wanderers" in Swahili). After a shakedown cruise of 1200 miles, Wes took off for Bocas del Toro, Panama, planning to pick up Sabine in Isla Mujeres, Mexico. But the voyage was cut short when Wes shipwrecked in violent seas off the western tip of Cuba and was rescued by the Carnival Cruise ship, VALOR.

When Wes abandoned ship he left behind all their possessions except their cat and his American flag. Immediately after the Coast Guard told Sabine of the rescue, she texted a friend a message that well defines the way these two live: "Boat lost at sea. Wes and crew alive. All possessions gone. New adventures ahead."

The couple rented a flat in a Mexican beach town for a few months, and then, on June 1st, 2011, they moved to Portland, Oregon to begin exploring America's Pacific Northwest. Their shopping list of replacement items included backpacks, a good knife, Merrill hiking boots, and of course, another adventure hat for Wes.

There is really no way to guess where the couple will be by the time you read this.

NOVELS BY WES DEMOTT, http://wesdemott.com

THE TYPHOON SANCTION

CIA Field Officer Cruiser is a master at manipulating people and circumstances. Be careful or he'll manipulate you in this story of vengeance, murder, and global terrorism.

Mixing spies and counterespionage with old vendettas and small town murders, The Typhoon Sanction pits the protagonist, CIA Agent Jay Stewart, against a Chinese enemy who hunts him halfway around the world to the Outer Banks of North Carolina. Stewart's mastery of misdirection provides a whodunit element to this international thriller as the reader tries to make sense of four mysterious small-town murders. The more obvious the truth appears, the further the reader gets from it, ultimately being captured by the same skills that made Stewart such a successful operative.

THE FUND

How deep does the conspiracy go? Who's in charge and how many more will die? Aerospace engineer Peter Jamison is determined to find out.

While trying to save his contract for a tactical weapons system, Jamison uncovers a crime of corruption, power and violence that draws him into a deadly game he cannot win but still chooses to fight, any way he can.

238

This thriller has been translated into several languages and is an international best-seller and IPPY Gold Medal Award Recipient for Best Fiction. Robert Ludlum, the wonderfully gracious man that he was, hosted the launch party for this novel.

HEAT SYNC

Heat Sync takes you through the U.S. Assassination School exposed by NEWSWEEK Magazine just prior to this novel's publication.

Experience the pain and process of sanctioned murder from Lt. Henry Thompson, who was recruited for JASPERS from the U.S. Navy SEALS. Thompson believes he's training to assassinate foreign threats to this country, and it's only after he graduates and gets his orders that he realizes his true mission is to kill the President of the United States by using the White House access his girlfriend provides, and that he's already too boxed in by his handlers to refuse. Heat Sync provides an exciting but non-traditional thriller that deeply probes the emotions and psychology of a patriotic killer.

WALKING K

America's leaders haven't faced a Prisoner-of-War crisis since the debacle over POWs left behind in Vietnam. Walking K is an exciting thriller that exposes the reasons it can't be allowed to happen again.

239

DeMott, a former FBI Agent, analyzed intelligence documents, Nixon's White House tapes, Congressional Records, and interviewed POWs and their commanding officers while researching this tragic story of a reluctant conspiracy lumbered upon the shoulders of each U.S. President since 1975. Crosscutting between dramatic battlefield scenes, heartbreaking torture, American businesses protecting their investments, and a continuing refusal by the White House to reveal the shameful truth, the emotional ending of this thriller sadly shows why the United States Government stopped wanting the prisoners of that war to come home, and perhaps sheds light on the government's attitude toward the POW classification in wars since Vietnam.

LOVING ZELDA

The humanity and hope of this beautiful novel makes it the work for which Wes would most like to be remembered. Loving Zelda's emotional range includes pieces of everyone's past, and provides hope that we can all find love if we're brave enough to take a chance. Loving Zelda is an extremely rare glimpse of the soft-as-cotton heart of internationally known tough guy Wes DeMott.

Loving Zelda explores the emotional pain and damage inflicted on a writer's relationship with the woman he loves as she struggles with manic-depression. Through ten years of joy and hardship he loves and cares for her with unwavering devotion, but when she marries another man he becomes a recluse on his sailboat, waiting for a chance to be together again in this or any world.

TORTUGA GOLD

Throw your sea bag aboard WASAFIRI to join Taz Keaton and the Mayday Salvage and Rescue gang in fun adventures and a chance at Blackbeard's treasure.

Tortuga Gold is a fun action story that follows Taz's fast adventures after he rejects his wealthy lifestyle and starts Mayday Salvage and Rescue in search of excitement. After Taz and his two partners race the Panamanian National Police to recover a metal case from the wreckage of a private jet in a muddy river, they meet a man with a coin from an historic but never recovered Spanish shipment that vanished in 1715. From there the adventure rolls from modern day pirates to blood-sucking leeches, exploding yachts to beautiful international competitors and a sea battle with the legendary Blackbeard himself. This is the first novel in a series involving Taz and the Mayday crew.

COMING SOON

TEQUILA BOOM BOOM

After enjoying your thrill ride with Taz Keaton and the Mayday gang in TORTUGA GOLD, join them on another adventure in TEQUILA BOOM BOOM.

www.ingramcontent.com/pod-product-compliance
Lightning Source LLC
Chambersburg PA
CBHW070605130626
46556CB00001B/272